Praise for
EMILY OUT OF FOCUS

"A heartfelt story exploring the complexities of family and friendship. Emily is so relatable, she flies right off the page and straight into your heart."

—Abby Cooper, author of *Sticks & Stones*
and *Bubbles*

"This story honestly relates the joy and struggle of a family as they pick up their long-awaited daughter from an orphanage in YiYang City in China. Readers will cheer Emily on as she transforms from a reluctant big sister and trepidatious traveler who is harboring a few secrets to a welcoming big sister."

—Hillary Homzie, author of *Apple Pie Promises*
and *Queen of Likes*

"A true-to-life story about one family's joys and struggles during the overseas adoption process."

—*Kirkus Reviews*

EMILY
OUT OF
FOCUS

Also by Miriam Spitzer Franklin
Extraordinary
Call Me Sunflower

EMILY OUT OF FOCUS

MIRIAM SPITZER FRANKLIN

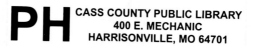

PH CASS COUNTY PUBLIC LIBRARY
400 E. MECHANIC
HARRISONVILLE, MO 64701

Sky Pony Press
New York

Sky Pony Press books may be purchased in bulk at special discounts for sales promotion, corporate gifts, fund-raising, or educational purposes. Special editions can also be created to specifications. For details, contact the Special Sales Department, Sky Pony Press, 307 West 36th Street, 11th Floor, New York, NY 10018 or info@skyhorsepublishing.com.

Sky Pony® is a registered trademark of Skyhorse Publishing, Inc.®, a Delaware corporation.

Visit our website at www.skyponypress.com.

10 9 8 7 6 5 4 3 2 1

Library of Congress Cataloging-in-Publication Data is available on file.

Cover design by Kate Gartner
Cover illustration by Jennifer Bricking

Print ISBN: 978-1-5107-3854-6
Ebook ISBN: 978-1-5107-3857-7

Printed in the United States of America

To my daughter, Carissa, with love

EMILY
OUT OF
FOCUS

CHAPTER ONE

April 2, 2014

Dear Diary,

I can't believe it! Tomorrow morning, in approximately six hours to be exact, we're leaving for China. And guess what? I am totally and completely wide awake. My stomach is swirling like a tornado, and even though I close my eyes, my mind keeps going and going.

So far, I've:

a) Gone into the kitchen to eat a granola bar and drink a glass of milk

b) Tried to make my body parts fall asleep, starting with my toes, the way Mom taught me the last time I was up worrying (Trust me, you do not want to put your toes to sleep while the rest of your body is wide awake. This method does NOT work unless the goal is to jump out of bed and stomp around on your pins-and-needle feet)

c) Checked to make sure I remembered to pack
   Nana's camera at the bottom of my bag where
   Mom and Dad won't see it (I did this while I was
   up stomping around on my tingly feet)
d) Turned on my radio since music used to help
   me sleep when I was little but turned it back
   off after singing along to three songs in a
   row.

I sighed and stared at my clock as the numbers turned to
12:00. Midnight. The last time I had such a bad case of not-
being-able-to-sleepitis was the night before I started middle
school. I'd gotten up and written down my fears in my journal, and I'm not sure why, but somehow that worked. Either
that or exhaustion finally set in. So, I turned to a fresh page in
my journal and wrote:

   MY FEARS ABOUT THE CHINA TRIP
   1) What if the plane crashes?
   2) What if authentic Chinese food means the
      food will be terribly awful and I starve the
      whole time?
   3) What if Mom and Dad find out I'm bringing
      Nana's camera?
   4) What if something happens to our luggage
      and I lose both Nana's camera... and
      PuddleDuck? (Okay, so maybe most twelve-
      year-olds don't sleep with a stuffed animal
      but I've had PuddleDuck since I was born, and
      I can't sleep without her!)

5) What if I don't like Katherine and I'm stuck hanging out with her for two weeks?

6) What if Mom and Dad want to spend most of the time in a hotel room once we get my new baby sister?

I chewed on my pen before writing the next question. It was something that had been worrying me ever since we got the news that we had a baby waiting for us in China, but it wasn't something I wanted to admit.

7) What if my new sister doesn't like me... and I don't care for her much either?

I stared down at the words I'd written, wishing I could cross them out. But I couldn't bring myself to do it because it was a real and genuine worry. I wasn't one of those girls who loved playing with babies, and I had no desire to change dirty diapers or hold a crying one-year-old. Besides, I was perfectly happy with my family exactly the way it was and becoming a big sister at age twelve seemed a little crazy to me.

But, we were leaving for China tomorrow and I could never share my feelings with my parents, who had acted like receiving the adoption referral was the best news they'd had in their whole entire lives.

I'd almost forgotten I was going to be a big sister. Back when my parents first told me, when I was five years old, I'd been so excited. I told everyone in my kindergarten class, and everyone in my first-grade class the next year, too. But by second grade, Mom and Dad stopped talking about it, at least in front of me, and I started thinking maybe it wasn't going to happen. Maybe they were thinking the same thing, too.

So, except for catching Mom looking at pictures of Waiting Children from China on the computer a couple of times, I had pushed the idea of being a big sister right out of my head. When we received the referral with a picture of a baby six months ago, it totally took me by surprise.

I read through my list one last time. The whole point about writing down your fears was that you had to be honest, so you could dump all your worries onto your paper and once you did that, you could stop thinking about them.

There. It was done. I shut my journal and tossed it into the bag I was carrying on the plane with me. Then I flopped back down on my bed, closing my eyes.

Next thing I knew, my alarm was buzzing loudly in my ears. "Time to get moving!" Dad called to me, flashing my light on and off. "Don't want to miss the trip of a lifetime!"

***

By the time we made it to the loading gate at JFK, my usually calm and organized parents were beginning to unravel, just like the hem of my jean shorts. They kept asking each other things like, "Do you have the blah blah this or did you remember to pack the blah blah that?" Apparently, there were a zillion details you had to take care of when you were adopting a baby, and if you forgot something important then when you got to China, they'd say, "Sorry, no baby for you!" I guess you could say my parents were about to crack under pressure.

"Just relax," Mom said to Dad, handing him a tissue. "We have plenty of time."

Dad mopped his forehead.

"Now take a few deep breaths," Mom said. "Like in yoga."

Dad breathed deeply, but he did not look like someone about to do a yoga pose. Actually, he looked more like a walking luggage rack. Our regular suitcases had been checked in, but Dad had a bunch of carry-on bags on each shoulder and an overstuffed backpack on his back. Every once in a while, we had to stop so he could readjust.

At first, I thought he was carrying all the bags because he had a lot of valuable things he didn't want to lose, like I was. But then Dad explained that we were over the weight limit and they'd charge a hefty fee if we tried to check any more luggage.

It was even worse once we got on the plane. It was like *Take a step, Bump, Take another step, Bump Bump . . .* Dad couldn't get down the aisle without knocking into someone. People shot us dirty looks. I think one man swore at us in

Chinese. Once we finally packed everything in the compartment above our heads, Dad sunk into his seat and let out a slow breath.

I let out a slow breath too. So . . . this was it. We were on our way to China. Like Dad said, it would be "the trip of a lifetime!"

And while my parents seemed to focus on adopting a baby, for me it was about so much more. It was my chance to prove I could be adventurous, like my grandmother had been. If I wanted to become a famous photojournalist someday too, then it was time to face my fears . . . starting with flying on a plane for twenty-one hours.

My stomach dropped. Twenty-one hours was a long time to be in the air, especially for someone who had never been on a plane before. And while I tried to think about how Nana would act if she was starting a journey across the ocean, all I could think about were the stories of plane crashes I'd heard about on the news.

A bell chimed, and to my surprise, an announcer spoke in rapid Chinese.

"We're off!" I shouted a few minutes later, trying my best to sound brave as the jets roared in my ears and the plane sped down the runway. We lifted into the sky, the world spreading out at a slant below us, the vehicles in the parking lot shrinking to the size of Matchbox cars. My stomach dropped as I realized we were getting farther and farther from the ground.

Millions of people fly every day, I told myself. Besides, it was time to get started on my adventure and my project. If I wanted to win a scholarship to the best photojournalism camp in the country, I needed to stay focused and not think about things like planes turning into fireballs in the midair.

So, I reached into my backpack and pulled out my digital camera. I figured once we got to China there'd be plenty of chances to use Nana's camera. Even though my parents had already given me the speech about being safe and not wandering off on my own in a foreign country, I had a feeling they'd be so busy chasing a new baby around that they wouldn't be able to watch my every move. And it's not like I was someone who got in trouble all the time. I was the type of kid a parent could trust.

Taking photos with Nana's camera—the one she'd used to take award-winning photos for *National Geographic* before she died of cancer a year ago—would give me the magic spark I needed. It would be as if she was standing right beside me, her spirit flowing from the camera to my hands.

What a great way to start my photo documentary—right here on the airplane! I shot pictures of the grass and trees and buildings below us, and when it turned into patches of browns and greens and grays, I took pictures of that, too. One thing

I'd learned from Nana—you had to take a lot of photos to get the perfect shot.

I pulled out a notebook and a green gel pen and was just getting started when the plane dipped. My stomach dipped too. The pen slid off my tray and landed on the floor. "What's going on?" I asked my mother.

"It's okay. I'm sure it's nothing," Mom said but her voice sounded a little weak. Dad had told me Mom was "an amateur flyer." By amateur, he meant that Mom wasn't very good at flying. I'd been afraid that I'd take after her, but so far, I was handling it better than she was.

The intercom buzzed. The pilot spoke in Chinese, lots of choppy words that seemed to go on for a paragraph.

"Mom!" I tugged at her sleeve and then I remembered what a friend from school had told me about her rocky plane ride. "I bet he said something about turbulence."

"Shh," my mother said. "Listen."

The pilot switched to English. His Chinese shrunk to a few short sentences. "We are experiencing turbulence. For your safety, remain in your seat. Fasten your seatbelts. Refrain from using the toilet at this time."

I picked up my pen and notebook and slipped them back into my bag, staring at the little white barf bags tucked into the seat in front of me. "Jenna had so much turbulence on her plane that she threw up." I wrinkled up my nose. "She said it was really gross, because not all the puke ended up in the bag."

Mom leaned back in her seat and closed her eyes.

"So how come we can't use the bathroom? If someone has to throw up—"

My mother groaned.

"Well, it's true. If you have to puke, it's a lot better to use the bathroom." I pulled the paper bag out of the seat in front of us.

Mom groaned again. "Can we please not talk about this?"

Dad laughed. "Lynn, you'll be okay. The turbulence will be over soon." He looked over at me. "You doing okay, Em?"

I took a big breath and nodded. The plane went *uuuup*, then dropped *downnn*. My ears popped. I stuck a piece of Cherry Bubblicious in my mouth. My mother was chewing at least three pieces of gum. She blew a big bubble with her eyes still closed.

Mom was starting to look green. Not green like grass. Green like the inside of a dill pickle.

"Do you want me to read to you?" I asked her. "I could read to you from my magazine about China if you want. There's all kinds of cool stuff we can do when we get there."

Mom shook her head. "How can you read with all this bumping around?"

I chomped down on my bubble gum. I didn't want to tell her that reading kept me from thinking about all the things that could go wrong on the plane, so I just said, "It's not bothering me much."

"Lucky," Mom said, squeezing my hand.

I squeezed back. I pulled out my magazine and tried to read it, but Mom was right. The words were bouncing around on the page. So I leaned back against my seat and closed my eyes. I didn't want to picture the plane, miles and miles from Earth bouncing around in the sky, and I didn't want to think about the baby, *my little sister*, waiting for us in China, either. So instead I thought about how exciting it would be if I won the contest and got to spend two weeks at the photojournalist camp in New York City.

I was most excited about getting to use the dark room to develop photos. Nana had already taught me all about adjusting the aperture and the shutter speed depending on the light. I could still picture her kind eyes behind her glasses, her patient voice as she answered my millions of questions, the way her face lit up after she returned from a photo shoot and couldn't wait to tell me all about it. She had often spoken about the art of photography and I knew she'd want me to have her real camera with me instead of a digital for the first of my world travels.

The up-and-down motion came to a stop. I heard a chiming sound and opened my eyes.

Dad patted my shoulder. "Look!" He pointed to the sign that read "BUCKLE YOUR SEATBELT AND REMAIN SEATED". It wasn't lit up anymore.

I looked over at my mother. "Did you hear that, Mom? No more turbulence! And you didn't even have to use a barf bag!"

"Hooray," Mom said. She cracked a smile that was still very green.

I got to work on a paragraph for the contest called "The Thrilling Plane Ride," then busied myself with doodle books and magazines for a while. I kept glancing at the map on the back of the seat in front of us, showing the flight in progress. So far, we'd been moving at the speed of an inchworm. It looked like it would take forever to get to China.

I was happy to find a movie about giant pandas, which kept me busy until a flight attendant came around with foil trays for supper. One of my goals was to take a photo of a giant panda while I was in China, even if I had to see one in a zoo instead of a rainforest.

"I'm starved!" I said, my stomach rumbling as I took the lid off my container and peered inside. A bunch of mixed-up stuff covered in a reddish sauce stared back at me. "What is it?" I asked my parents.

Dad poked his fork around, jabbed at something, and took a bite. "I think it's chicken. With vegetables and rice."

"What kind of vegetables?" I asked, because it didn't look like any vegetables I'd ever seen.

"Not sure exactly," Dad said, taking a bite.

"WAIT!" I yelled, suddenly remembering a conversation I'd had at school. "Don't eat anymore!"

Dad looked up at me. "What's wrong, Emily?"

"You need to ask about the ingredients." I lowered my voice. "It could be bugs."

Dad laughed. "What are you talking about?"

"Bugs. Insects. Like crickets or ants or grasshoppers—"

"Emily," my mother said, poking around in the container with her fork. "What in the world would make you think they're serving us *insects* for dinner?"

"Aviva Greenberger said they eat insects in China, and she's the smartest person in the sixth grade. Besides, I looked it up on the Internet and it's true. People like to eat fried bugs there. It's a delicacy."

"*Some* people consider it a delicacy," Mom said. "That doesn't mean that everyone in China eats bugs for every meal, and they certainly wouldn't serve it as a meal to travelers on an airplane."

Mom sounded like she knew what she was talking about, but I looked over at Dad to be sure.

"Of course they wouldn't," Dad said, taking a big bite to prove it. "Come on, Emily. Give it a try."

I stared down at my dinner. "Maybe we should ask a flight attendant."

Dad shook his head. "This is Air China and I'm quite sure it didn't say anything about serving insect delicacies."

"Gross," I said. I stuck my fork in the rice and took a tiny bite. It didn't seem too different from the Chinese food I'd eaten at Wang Fu's, but I examined each bite carefully, just to be sure.

After dinner came an exciting trip to the bathroom (what would happen if someone got stuck in the bathroom for ten hours or more?), and another movie, and about fifty pages into my new fantasy novel, the flight attendant dimmed the lights inside the plane. The sky outside had been dark for a while and I yawned then curled up on the seat with my head in Mom's lap and fell right asleep. Next thing I knew, someone was shaking me gently.

"Wake up sleepyhead," Dad said. "We're in China."

CHAPTER TWO

CHINA, DAY 1, 4/3/14

Dear Diary,

We made it! After twenty-one hours in the sky, I've survived my first plane ride! Now I'm on my way to becoming a seasoned flier just like Nana (instead of an amateur one, like Mom)!

The worst part was worrying about having to use a puke bag or getting locked in the bathroom while we were thousands of miles up in the sky. Luckily the turbulence stopped before any of us got sick and I solved the bathroom problem by making Mom stand outside the door and keeping it cracked just a bit. Dinner last night on the plane was an adventure because of the mystery food but this trip is all about adventure, right? And I can hardly wait to get started!

Love, Emily
(who has now conquered her fear of flying)

After I finished my journal entry, I flipped back a few pages and put a check mark next to #1 on My Fears About the China Trip: What if the plane crashes? One fear down, six more to go . . . and we'd only just arrived. I called that progress.

Dad was beginning to bark commands, so I snapped my journal shut and tossed it back in my bag.

"All right," Dad said. "Now everyone stick close together. You don't want to get lost in a crowded airport in a foreign country. No wandering off—"

"Dad," I said. "You've already told me a hundred times. No wandering, stick close together, pay attention—"

"Just checking to make sure." Dad readjusted a shoulder bag and took a deep breath. "Everyone ready?"

Mom and I both said, "Ready!" and we stepped out into the aisle, making our way into a crowded airport full of signs I couldn't read. As I listened to the hum of voices all around me, I realized I couldn't understand a single word.

I picked up my pace, making sure not to lose sight of my dad and his red backpack.

When we finally made it to the baggage area, I spotted our travel group right away. They were the only large group of non-Asian people I'd seen in the whole airport. A Chinese woman with long dark hair, large hoop earrings, and round glasses rushed over to us. She greeted us with a friendly smile. "You must be the Saunders family!" Holding up a clipboard, she pointed to a photo of our family. "I'm Lisa Wu from World Adoptions. The other families are waiting, too."

Lisa had a heavy accent, but I hung on every word. After my parents shook hands with the Dopps, Lisbons, and Sullivans, Lisa Wu introduced us to the Bresners.

A Chinese girl with shiny hair gathered in two French braids stood with her parents, and they all wore matching T-shirts with a photo of a baby on the front.

"This is Katherine Bresner," Lisa Wu said to me. I took a closer look. She wore a jean mini-skirt with a pink blouse tied at the bottom over her T-shirt. Polished pink toenails peeked out from white sandals. I glanced down at my rumpled Empire State Building T-shirt, wondering if she'd changed once she got off the plane. That's when I remembered I hadn't bothered to comb my hair, and I hadn't brushed my teeth, either. How had she managed to look so fresh and clean after flying on an airplane all night?

"Katherine was adopted from China when she was little," Lisa continued. "Now she's going to be a big sister, just like you!"

Giving my jean shorts a tug, I looked up and smiled at Katherine. She didn't smile back. But she started talking right away. "What's your sister's name?" Katherine asked me. For a moment, my mind froze. *My sister. The whole reason we were in China, right?*

"Her name?" Katherine repeated.

"Mei Lin," I said quickly.

"Do you know what it means?"

I shook my head.

"Well, it's pretty easy to find out." Katherine pulled a booklet from her bag and flipped through it. "It means Beautiful Lotus Flower."

"Oh. Thanks," I said. "What's your sister's name?"

"Ai Wen. It means Love Beautiful Cloud."

"Are you calling her Ai Wen . . . or Cloud?"

Katherine snorted. "Have you ever heard of anyone named Cloud?"

I shrugged. I'd only just met Katherine, but something about her made me feel like she was much older than me, even though we were both twelve.

"We're calling her neither. My sister's name is Madison." Katherine pointed to her T-shirt. In big letters were the words *Welcome Home, Ai Wen (Madison)*.

"Oh," I said. "We don't have any T-shirts of Mei Lin."

"My dad owns a screening shop, so he made lots of shirts to give away. We might have an extra, if you want."

"That's okay," I said. Why would I want a shirt with Katherine's sister on it? Sheesh. I wouldn't even wear a T-shirt that had Mei Lin's photo on it. I'd seen some of those adoption blogs that people posted and was glad my parents had a little sense about the whole thing. Either that, or they were overwhelmed enough with packing lists and just trying to get a room ready for a baby when it had been *twelve* years since they'd had one.

"Is your baby a Waiting Child?" Katherine asked me.

I shook my head. My parents had explained to me that a lot of adoptions these days were babies with special needs, known as Waiting Children. In the past, too many baby girls had ended up in orphanages, but a lot had changed since my parents started the adoption process. Now families in China were adopting a lot of the girls without special needs, which is why we'd waited so long to be matched with Mei Lin.

"Why not?" Katherine asked me. "We only had to wait a year for Madison. She has a cleft palate. It's an opening in her lip, see?" She pointed to her T-shirt, but I couldn't see it very clearly. "She'll have surgery when we bring her home, and then she'll be just fine."

I shrugged. I didn't really know my parents' reasons for not choosing a Waiting Child. They were adult reasons, and they were complicated. Katherine sure was nosy! "So," I asked, switching the subject, "have you ever been to China before?"

"Katherine raised one eyebrow at me. I cleared my throat. "I mean, after you were adopted?"

"This is the second time I've been back," Katherine said as she flipped a braid over her shoulder. I imagined what I looked like, my hair probably sticking out like coiled springs all around my head. Before I fell asleep, I'd taken out the elastic that usually held back my unruly curly hair and hadn't bothered to put it back in. I had a feeling Katherine noticed.

I was relieved when an announcement came over the intercom and I didn't have to keep trying to make conversation. A man spoke in fast Chinese. I was about to ask Lisa Wu what it meant when Katherine said, "The luggage from our flight is ready."

I stared at her. "You speak Chinese?"

"Sure. I go to the Chinese Immersion School in San Francisco. Actually, the official language of China is *Mandarin*, not Chinese."

Mrs. Bresner, who'd been talking to my parents, turned to me. "Katherine's been fluent in Mandarin since first grade."

Mandarin, Chinese, it made no difference to me. All I knew is people spoke it really fast and I didn't understand a word. I was impressed that Katherine spoke a language that seemed so different from ours, but I wasn't about to tell her that.

"Now we'll know who to take with us to the restaurants," Dad said as we headed to the luggage turnstile, which actually made Katherine smile for the first time.

This time I was the one who didn't smile back. I wasn't sure how much I wanted to hang out with Katherine. I'd been hopeful about having another girl my age on the trip, but after knowing her for only a few minutes, it was easy to tell we weren't about to become great friends. We were too different.

Once we'd picked up our suitcases, all of us piled into a large blue van. Lisa called it a van, anyway. It looked more like a small bus. Two seats hugged each side of the aisle, so my parents and I headed to the bench across the back. Lisa stood at the front with a microphone so she could speak over the huge fans that rattled as it clunked down the highway.

"The Dolton Hotel is in the middle of Changsha," Lisa Wu told us. "We'll be there in approximately forty-five minutes. You'll have the afternoon to do whatever you like and get your paperwork in order. If I were you, I'd get some rest. Because tomorrow, you will get your babies!"

Everyone around me cheered when she said that. The word *tomorrow* echoed in my ears.

I looked down at my hands clasped together in my lap. Today I was still an only child. But tomorrow, I'd become a big sister.

Everything was about to change.

'We pulled out of the airport, passing big green fields and swampy rice paddies until we turned onto the interstate. Lisa Wu chattered on and on about the city and its people. I glanced over at Katherine who stared out the window in awe, as if the groups of old brick apartment buildings with green vines growing on the sides were the most fascinating thing she'd ever seen.

Hopefully when we got to Changsha there would be more to look at because the view from the highway didn't offer great possibilities for my photo documentary. And my photos had to be amazing if I wanted to win a scholarship to one of the best photojournalism camps in the country.

Like Nana said, if you really wanted to be good at something, you had to learn your craft. *"You must listen to experts in the field,"* she'd told me, *"and learn to take constructive criticism. You have to stretch your boundaries and do things you never thought you could."*

By boundaries, she meant that she traveled all over the world. And I was taking the first step now, at age twelve, by traveling to China. This trip was the opportunity I'd been waiting for—the chance to impress those judges and win the contest, and then my parents would let me go to photojournalism camp instead of forcing me to go to those Math and STEM camps like they did last summer.

Building things in STEM wasn't so bad, but ever since I took a test in second grade that said I excelled in math, my parents kept talking about how I could become an engineer or doctor someday. If I won the contest, they'd finally take me seriously, instead of thinking photography was just another hobby like collecting trading cards or taking a yoga class or something.

"Look, Emily, we're in downtown Changsha!" Dad said. I tuned back in just as we turned onto a busy four-lane road. Tall skyscrapers appeared right in front of me. I stared out at sidewalks crowded with small shops selling their products on the street tucked between tall shiny buildings covered with billboards of beautiful models. I recognized a KFC and McDonalds that looked exactly like the ones we had at home except for the characters on the sign.

I'm not sure exactly what I had been expecting, but this wasn't it. Workers with white hats standing in rice paddies as the airplane flew in for a landing—that wasn't so surprising. All the photos of China I'd seen boasted beautiful mountains and lakes, forests filled with giant panda bears and wild tigers, multi-leveled ancient pagodas. But a city that looked a lot like New York?

I leaned forward in my seat to get a better look. Cars whizzed by honking their horns. Motorcycles and motor scooters and green taxi cabs weaved in and out, barely missing us as they switched lanes. Then, in the middle of it all, I spotted an old man slowly pedaling a bike, wearing a straw hat, pulling a cart full of vegetables.

So, maybe it was a little different from New York City after all.

What was I waiting for? I pulled out my digital and began snapping photos as fast as I could.

CHAPTER THREE

"This is our home for the next week," Dad said as we entered the lobby of the grandest hotel I'd ever been to in my entire life. "Can you believe it?"

Sparkling lights hung like diamonds from high ceilings. Shiny floors surrounded a fountain, the water exploding into bubbles. Off to the side stretched a row of shops like you'd see in a fancy mall.

"There's a swimming pool and a bowling alley," Lisa Wu said. "And don't forget the baby playrooms on the tenth and eleventh floor."

"Baby playroom?" my mom asked, more interested in that than anything else Lisa had mentioned.

Lisa nodded. "A lot of people stay at the Dolton when they're adopting, so the hotel has a nice place for everyone to go with their children."

"Wow!" I said, taking in the sights.

"Can we go swimming this afternoon?" Katherine asked her parents.

"We're going to The Provincial Museum, remember?" Mrs. Bresner said.

"Oh. Yeah," Katherine said. Her voice dropped as if she was disappointed but then she brightened. "It's going to be really cool, with mummies and everything."

I glanced over at my parents. "Can we go, too?"

Dad shook his head right away. "There's plenty of time for sightseeing."

"Aww, come on," I begged. "Katherine's family's going."

Dad lowered his voice. "We'll discuss it in the room," he said firmly, and I knew what that meant. I groaned, but I waited until we made it to the seventh floor. As grand as the lobby was, I expected a humongous room. But it was small and plain, with two double beds close to each other and a small TV set.

"I guess the crib will have to go here," Mom said, pointing to the bit of open area near the windows.

I pulled back the curtains and stared at the tall buildings that stood out against a hazy sky. "You heard what Lisa

Wu said," I told my parents. "We're going to pick up Mei Lin tomorrow. I think we should go sightseeing baby-free like Katherine's family, while we still have a chance."

"I believe Lisa's advice was to use the time to rest." Mom yawned. "I, for one, plan to take her up on it. You might have had a good night's sleep, but I don't think I slept for all of five minutes."

"You mean . . . you're going to take a nap?" I watched as my mother kicked off her shoes and stretched out on the bed. "When there's so many exciting things to do?"

Dad laughed. "We both need a nap, but I'll take you to the pool in a little while, okay?"

I sighed in exasperation as Dad collapsed on the bed next to Mom.

"Katherine's parents don't need naps," I said.

"Katherine's parents are not *your* parents," Dad said in a tone that told me the conversation was officially over.

I could not believe we had traveled clear across the world and I was stuck in a hotel room with parents who were going to spend the afternoon sleeping. "Well . . . can I at least explore the hotel?"

"No," both of my parents said at the same time.

"Why not? I can take your cell phone."

"Because we're in a foreign country," Mom said, as if that were enough of an explanation.

"But—"

"No buts about it, Emily," Dad said. "I'm just going to take a quick nap, and then we'll go swimming and we'll explore the hotel. Together, okay?"

"Whatever," I said, crossing my arms in front of my chest. Mom rolled over and ignored me, which was weird because she didn't usually let me get away with a sassy tone like that.

"I'm waking you up in thirty minutes."

"Forty-five," Dad said.

I let out another big sigh and threw in a *Hmph!* which didn't even get a reaction from my parents. There was nothing adventurous about this at all! Our one chance to get out and do exciting things without a crying baby, and all Mom and Dad could focus on was catching a few Zzzzs. You'd think a history professor and a middle school social studies teacher would be a little more interested in seeing living, breathing history.

I'd studied the schedule with my parents before we left, asking if we'd be able to do things outside of the group. "Of course, Emily!" Mom and Dad had said with enthusiasm. "We'll be in China for two whole weeks. There will be plenty of time to see all the things we want to."

Well, it looked like their excited words had been swallowed right up by the Changsha skyline. Mom and Dad seemed exhausted from the plane ride, and maybe it had finally hit them: they were going to be the new parents of a squirmy, crying eighteen-month-old.

A loud buzzing noise interrupted my thoughts. I turned away from the window and, sure enough, the sounds were coming from my dad, who was already snoring away.

That's it! Just because my parents weren't interested in adventures didn't mean I had to spend my time listening to them snooze in a hotel room.

If I stepped outside of the room for a few minutes, how would they ever know? I tore a sheet of paper out of my notebook and wrote a quick note: Went to check out the baby playroom. Took Dad's cell phone. Be back in five minutes. Emily

Then I closed the blinds, darkening the room so if my parents did wake up, they might think it was the middle of the night and not even look around for me. But if they did look around for me in the next few minutes, they'd see my note . . . and it would be okay. They couldn't get angry if I told them I was exploring the baby playroom just down the hall. What could possibly be dangerous about that? Besides, they liked anything that had the word BABY in it.

I went back and added *Love* in front of my name and drew a few hearts. Just in case. Then I slipped my dad's cell phone and the hotel key into my backpack with Nana's camera safely inside and tiptoed out of the room. The door closed with a click behind me.

For a minute, I stared out at the empty hallway, my hand still on the doorknob. It was completely quiet, except for the sounds of my heart beating loudly in my chest. I knew it was partly from excitement, since I was someone who usually followed the rules. But that wasn't the only reason.

I was about to go off by myself, in a foreign country where hardly anyone seemed to speak English. All kinds of scary possibilities raced through my mind.

Nana's voice echoed in my head. *"Take chances. Don't be afraid to fail. Break a few rules. That's what you have to do if you want to chase after your dreams."*

I was pretty sure my parents wouldn't have approved if they'd heard her give me that advice. And I'm pretty sure Nana wasn't suggesting I disobey my parents. But I was also pretty sure that a trip without adventure meant I'd never get the photos I'd need to prove myself as a photojournalist.

And since no one was watching me, this was the perfect opportunity to snap some great pictures with Nana's camera!

So, I tried to block out my worries and what-ifs, walking straight to the elevator instead of stopping at the playroom at the end of the hall.

When I stepped out in the lobby, I drew in my breath, taking in the bubbling fountain and the sparkling chandeliers. I'd already taken photos of the lobby with my digital, but I took a few with Nana's before tossing a few coins into the fountain for good luck. Then I headed straight for the first gift shop to my right, Jai-lu's Treasures.

Tea sets, vases, fans, and artwork filled the shelves. Baskets sat on the floor full of little cloth bags, dolls, books, and hats of all colors. Red lanterns hung from the ceiling. I used Nana's camera to snap some more pictures.

As I headed over to watch an artist in the back of the shop, I heard my dad's cell phone ring. My heart thumped. I pulled the cell phone out of my pocket quickly, the way you pull off a Band-Aid so it won't hurt. Whew! It wasn't Mom's cell calling, just some number I didn't recognize. I slipped the phone back in my pocket and turned to the artist.

The man was sticking a paintbrush into a hole in a little glass ball. The writing showed up on the outside. "Wow! How do you do that?" I asked, not even stopping to wonder if he could understand what I had said.

Luckily, the artist spoke English. He looked up at me and smiled. "Simple," he said. "Just takes practice."

"That is so cool." Gumball-sized spheres decorated with pictures of animals sat in a tray on the counter. "Did you paint the pictures too?"

The man nodded. "You pick. You like a panda bear?" He held one up for me to take a closer look.

"I love it," I said. "What are you writing on the outside?"

"Your name. Birthday. Whatever you want me to write."

"Ohh, that is so awesome."

"Is only 35 yuan. Is cheaper for a nice girl like you."

"I'll have to come back later," I said. "With my parents."

The man nodded and got back to work. "You come back. I give a good price."

"Okay," I said. I didn't want to push my luck, so I headed out of the store. As I reached the door, I felt someone pull my ponytail. I spun around quickly.

A woman stood behind me, holding up her camera and smiling. A little boy of about five or six stood by her side. She pointed to me, then to the camera. She motioned for me to come closer.

I shook my head and raced out of the store. The lady didn't exactly look threatening. I mean, she was a mom and everything, but why would a total stranger want *my* photo?

A little taste of adventure was probably enough for one afternoon. I ran to the elevator and mashed the button on the elevator. As I waited, I felt someone run a hand down my hair.

I whipped around. There was the same lady, still holding up her camera!

Shivers ran up and down my arms. I shook my head again, my cheeks heating up. She had followed me from the store to the elevator. Alarm bells set off in my head. This was one of those situations my parents had tried to warn me about! One of the reasons why I shouldn't have been wandering off alone in a foreign country!

I ran away from the elevator as the doors were opening and raced up seven flights of stairs, not stopping until I landed in front of my hotel room. I opened the door as quick as I could, shutting it hard behind me.

Leaning against it, I closed my eyes tight and tried to catch my breath.

"Emily?" came Dad's voice from the bed. "Is that you?"

CHAPTER FOUR

Dad sat up and rubbed his eyes. "What was that noise?"

I stepped away from the door, trying to make a quick recovery. "Noise?" I repeated. "What noise?"

"It sounded like someone came in the door."

"Oh, that noise." *Think fast, Emily.* I opened the door, then closed it again so it clicked. "Is that what you heard?"

"Emily." Dad no longer sounded half-asleep. "We told you not to leave the room, am I correct?"

"Sure, Dad. I heard sounds in the hall. So, I opened the door to see what it was."

"And . . . what was it?"

"Nothing. Just some people walking by."

"Hmph," Dad said.

"Are we going swimming now?" I asked. As I glanced around the room, I spied my note on the desk, clearly saying I'd stepped outside of the room for a few minutes. If Dad got up and saw it, I was dead. "Or do you want to sleep a few more minutes?" I said quickly.

Dad gave me a suspicious look. He frowned and squinted, but that could have been because I looked blurry when he didn't have his glasses on. "You're not in a hurry to get to the pool?"

I shook my head. "I need to work on my journalism entry for Day One. For the contest, remember?"

Dad had a dazed expression on his face. I didn't know if he'd forgotten about the contest or if he was still half-asleep. Last month I'd shown him the entry form I found in my *Adventure Girls* magazine, and I'd been talking about it ever since. But whenever I talked to him about it, I got the idea his mind was busy thinking about other things and he wasn't really listening.

"Ten more minutes," he mumbled, rolling back over on the bed. I wished he'd sat up and asked me what I was going to write about, or what pictures I planned to include. *Oh, well,* I thought as I watched him fall back asleep in about two seconds. At least I knew he hadn't paid much attention to the story I told him about opening and closing the door.

I put the cell back where I'd found it. Then I picked up my note, tearing it into shreds before throwing it in the trashcan underneath some tissues. I would make a seriously good spy.

Plugging in my laptop, I tried to decide what to write about. I pulled out the contest directions and read them over for the umpteenth time:

Tell a story with photos and words. You may use up to 15 photos and 1000 words.

Your entry will be judged on creativity, composition, and style. Your goal is to effectively combine photography and writing to make a powerful statement about your topic.

Problem was, I had no idea what kind of statement I wanted to make. So far, all I knew was that China seemed different from what I had expected.

MY TRIP TO CHINA
By Emily Rose Saunders

For over twenty hours, we flew on a plane that crossed over land and oceans. It would take me to a country that was very different from my own.

I sat back and read my beginning. Not bad, though I needed a much catchier title. I twirled a strand of hair around my finger, thinking about what to write next. When nothing came to me, I decided instead to make a list of the photos I had so far:

1) Clouds outside the airplane window
2) Traffic in Changsha
3) Changsha's skyline
4) Lobby of The Dolton Hotel
5) The artist painting glass balls

Hmmm. I didn't see anything too exciting about my list and wasn't sure how I could link them together to make a powerful statement. Maybe I needed to wait until I printed the photos and an amazing idea would come to me. My mind was a complete blank about what to write, so I shut down the computer and woke up my dad.

"You can't sleep all day!" I said, shaking his shoulders.

Mom made a sleepy noise and rolled over. Dad stretched and got to his feet. First thing he did was check his cell phone. "I must have been out cold. I didn't even hear it ring."

"You were snoring away. I even turned on the TV and it didn't wake you up," I fibbed. "So, did they leave a message?"

Dad held the phone to his ear. "It's Lisa. She said all the families are meeting at the restaurant next door for dinner tonight."

"Katherine, too?"

"Unless they're too worn out from their trek to the Great Wall," Dad said with a grin.

"The Great Wall? I thought you said we couldn't go because it was at the other end of the country."

"It is. I was just kidding." Dad dug around in the suitcase for his swim trunks. "So, was anything on?"

I stared at him, trying to figure out what he meant.

"On TV. You said you were watching while we were asleep."

"Oh." I shook my head. "It was all in Chinese," I said. As soon as the words popped out of my mouth I wanted to turn on the TV to see if I was right. But I wasn't too worried about Mom and Dad catching me in a lie. They could probably go for two weeks without even noticing the TV was in our room.

Dad and I swam for a while in the hotel pool and soon it was time to meet the other families for dinner. Mom had wasted the whole afternoon napping and unpacking, but she looked happy as could be as we headed downstairs.

Lisa Wu and the other families were already in the front of the restaurant, waiting for a table. Katherine wore a yellow sundress and sandals, her hair in a perfect French braid with a yellow ribbon woven throughout. I glanced down at my shorts and T-shirt and ran a hand over my lopsided ponytail. I'd changed into clean clothes after swimming, but after taking a look at Katherine, I felt underdressed.

"How are you?" Lisa asked us. "Did you have a good and restful afternoon?"

"Wonderful," Mom said.

"The Provincial Museum was fabulous," Mrs. Bresner said. "We spent the whole afternoon there, but we didn't see half of it."

"Yes, it's a very good museum," Lisa agreed. "You should visit, too, Emily. You will like it there."

I glanced over at Mom and Dad. "I told my parents I wanted to go—"

"We had a lot to do," Mom said quickly. "Getting settled after such a long trip."

"Oh, of course," Lisa said. "Maybe on one of your other days in Changsha you will have more time."

"What did you do this afternoon?" Katherine asked me while the grown-ups chatted.

"Went swimming," I said.

"Well, the museum was great," Katherine said, and then she talked nonstop about it, telling me in great detail about every exhibit on every floor. Finally, the waitress led us to a large round table, and Katherine took the seat right next to me.

I studied the menu. I couldn't read the words, so I studied the large color photos instead. Which didn't help one bit.

"Don't they have chow mein?" I whispered to my mother, not wanting Katherine to hear.

Mom shook her head. "That's more of an American dish," she said. "I'll ask Lisa to order something for us."

Lisa had a long conversation with the waiter, so I hoped that meant she was ordering something good. When the food arrived, I recognized the white rice. That's about it. Lisa explained there were bowls of vegetables, chicken, seafood, fried bean curd, even snake. But what got me was that in the middle of it all sat a big plate of . . . DUCK. Peking Duck, to be exact.

I gulped. It's not that it looked like a real duck, with a head and feathers or anything. It just looked like roasted meat. But once Lisa told us what it was, I couldn't help thinking about it. When I was little, ducks were my favorite animal in the world. Every weekend we used to go to the park so I could feed the ducks at the pond. I was trying to act very casual about that dead duck sitting smack in the middle of our table, but Dad saw right through me.

"Just pretend it's chicken," Dad said with a grin. "That's what I'm going to do with the snake."

I frowned. "But it's not," I said, thinking about the collection of duck stuffed animals sitting on my bed and the little china ducks on my dresser. I glanced over at Katherine, who was spooning a helping from each dish onto her plate. She even took some of the duck. Then she picked up her chopsticks and started to eat.

"Where are the forks?" I whispered to my parents.

Dad shrugged. "If it's not broke, don't fix it," he said, picking up a pair of chopsticks.

"What's that supposed to mean?" I asked him.

"It means this particular utensil has worked for the Chinese for thousands of years. So, you may as well give it a try. Here I'll show you."

It didn't look like I had a choice, so I picked up a pair, trying to slant the sticks and hold them between my fingers the way Dad was doing. Then I took a better look at the dishes that sat in the middle of the table on a spinning server. It didn't look like any of the food I'd seen at Chinese restaurants at home. The sauces were different, and all of the dishes had green leafy vegetables that looked suspiciously like seaweed.

I figured I could skip most of it and settle for rice, but I didn't see any little red-capped bottles on the table like we always had at Wan Fu's. "Where's the soy sauce?" I asked Mom.

She shook her head. "It's different here. Just use some of the sauce from the dishes."

I made a face. Whoever heard of rice without soy sauce? My stomach rumbled, and that's when I remembered my Fears About the China Trip. It was time to face the one I'd written about food, so I summoned my courage and took a helping of everything, except the snake *and* the duck, of course.

The biggest thing on my plate was a chunk of fried bean curd. Wrinkling my nose, I grabbed a piece and squeezed tight enough to keep it between the chopsticks as I lifted it from the plate. But just as I opened my mouth, the sticks shifted and the tofu dropped out.

I went for the soy sauce-less rice next. At least it was familiar. I scraped it between the sticks, squeezed them together, lifted it to my mouth . . . and the rice fell back onto the plate.

I tried again, using my fingers to pick up a bigger scoop. But I couldn't keep it between the sticks. I was about to grab a handful and plop it in my mouth when Katherine giggled.

"Have you actually eaten anything yet?" she asked.

"I'm doing just fine, thank you very much," I told her. What I needed was a new strategy. I studied the chopsticks carefully. There had to be an easier way. I tuned out the snippets of conversation going on around the table, concentrating so hard I dropped a stick and it clanked against the plate. That's when it came to me. A chopstick would make a very good spear! Everything could be stabbed with a stick, except for rice. I'd have to give up on that.

I wasn't crazy about the strange flavors—some spicy, some sweet, some hard to define, and I was having to pick around things I didn't recognize—but at least I managed to get the food in my mouth. I was munching away, spearing the food and pulling it off the chopstick with my teeth, when Lisa noticed.

"Here, let me help you." She showed me the correct way to hold the sticks against my thumb, using my pointer finger to pick up the food.

"Thanks," I told her, "but my way works for me." I speared another chunk of chicken and swallowed it down.

Lisa Wu shook her head. "Never stab the food," she told me. "And never hold the chopsticks straight up and down on your plate."

"Why not?"

"Stabbing is not polite. Is disrespectful. If you hold the chopsticks up and down, people think it is a funeral pyre."

Katherine snorted. I felt my cheeks flare. I had no idea what a pyre was, but I wasn't about to ask. Funerals were high on my list of Things You Shouldn't Think About. I immediately slanted my chopsticks in the right direction before anyone else at the table noticed.

It wasn't as easy as she'd made it look. My fingers were too clumsy or something. And for all that hard work, the food kept falling off the sticks and landing back on my plate, all squished out of shape.

After a while, Mom nudged me in the side. "Here," she said, pulling a plastic fork out of her purse. "It takes a while to learn to use chopsticks. By the time we leave here, you'll be a real pro."

Katherine gave me a *"You are so pitiful, using that fork"* look and I shot her a dirty look back. I'd managed pretty well for my first time, after all. In about five minutes, I had finished off all my rice and had picked out a few other food morsels as well, which ended up tasting surprisingly good.

I was slurping from a large slab of watermelon the server had passed out after the meal when Katherine leaned in close to me and whispered, "I have a secret."

At first, I thought I was hearing things, but when I looked over at her she smiled. "And I want you to help me with it."

I just stared at her. We hadn't exactly become BFFs, but all anyone ever had to do is say the word "*secret*" and I was in. "You want *me* to help you?"

She looked around the table at the grown-ups, then said, "I'll tell you later, when we're alone."

I raised my eyebrows, and she put a finger to her lips. Before I could try to find out anything else, Lisa began telling everyone what to pay. Soon after, we left the restaurant.

When we returned to our room, I was feeling pretty happy about the fact that I'd eaten my first authentic Chinese meal and survived. In two weeks, I'd be able to check off something else on my list of fears. Then I started thinking about Katherine's secret, wondering what she meant by needing my help, and that's when I noticed the crib.

It stood at the end of the room, near the window. I froze next to the desk while my dad walked over to examine it.

"Not bad," Dad said. He jiggled the railing and slid it down. "Might take a little practice though—it looks like it's been through some wear and tear. Lynn, you want to give it a try?"

I looked over at Mom. She had sunk down on the edge of the bed and wasn't moving.

"Mom . . . are you all right?"

She just stared at the crib.

"I bet it's easy." I walked over and squeezed the latch. Then I jiggled it like Dad did, but the rail didn't budge.

"Needs a parents' magic touch," Dad said, sliding it smoothly again. Then he looked over at my mom. "Lynn? Are you okay?"

Mom shook her head. "It's really happening," she said in a quiet voice.

I sat down next to her. Mom's eyes were full of tears. "Mom? What's wrong?"

She shook her head and put her arms around me. She laid her cheek against my hair.

"Your mother's just happy," Dad said. "We've waited a long time for your little sister."

I thought about that for a minute. Whoever heard of having a second baby when an only child had worked out great for twelve years? I knew my parents had been on a waiting list for a long time, but when exactly did they decide I wasn't enough? "Did you cry when I was born?"

Mom wiped her eyes and smiled. "Yes, Emily, I certainly did. Your father cried, too."

"You did?" I looked over at Dad. "I don't believe it. Did you *really* cry?"

Dad nodded, then broke into a grin. "Only because it meant the end of milkshakes every night. Did you know it was doctor's orders?"

"Daddy! It was doctor's orders for Mom." I'd heard the story a million times. The doctor didn't think I was growing enough. So he told Mom to stay in bed and eat lots of ice cream for six weeks.

"It's never any fun to eat ice cream alone," Dad said. "But it's a good thing you came when you did. I was starting to look like I was the one who was going to have a baby. Just like this." He stuck a pillow under his shirt and paraded around the room.

I giggled. Soon we were all laughing, even Mom. For a moment I forgot what the crib really meant. But as I glanced over at it, I remembered. And I stopped laughing.

Mom and Dad and I fit together just right. Three was the perfect number for our family. But tomorrow, we would become a family of four.

CHAPTER FIVE

China, DAY 2, 4/4/14

Dear Diary,
We just got back from the breakfast buffet at the Dolton Hotel. You can find everything in the world spread across long tables: pancakes and waffles, muffins and breads, cereal and yogurt, fresh fruit, bowls of hot soup and noodles. I also saw platters with weird slimy things: eel? worms? jellyfish? I decided not to ask.

My parents told me to eat up because it's going to be a long morning at the government buildings, so I did. Hopefully they don't know what they're talking about. I mean, how long can it take to hand out babies?

The truth is, I'm worried about this big-sister thing. I know I've had YEARS to get used to it, but I never thought it would really happen. Well in a little while we are going to meet her, and we'll never be able to go back to our family the way it is now.

So, I have this rotten feeling in the pit of my stomach, like I actually ate some of those slimy things on the buffet bar, and they are squirming around inside of me. Because I know I'm supposed to be excited about being a big sister, but instead I'm thinking about everything that will be different. And that makes me feel like a spoiled five-year-old instead of a mature twelve-year-old who welcomes new adventures.

Love,
Emily
(who is trying to get rid of negative thoughts and be the person my parents think she is)

Soon it was time to load up the van. Lisa Wu stood in front again with the microphone. At first, she talked about boring things like paperwork. I stared out the window at the rainy day, not even listening. Until she started to sing.

"Crawfish pie, jum-ba-lai me oh my oh!"

I clapped a hand over my mouth, so I wouldn't burst out laughing. Not only was it the silliest song I had ever heard, but Lisa Wu *could not sing*. I'm not sure what the tune was supposed to be, but I was pretty sure it wasn't the tune I was hearing. I looked up at Dad. He grabbed my hand and squeezed it. I could tell he was trying very hard not to crack a smile.

I glanced over at Katherine. Her hair was braided and twirled in two coils on both sides of her head, and she wore a red sundress with little white flowers all over it. I'd gotten used to the fact that she liked to dress like she was in a fashion show every day, but how did her mom have time for a fancy hairstyle on a morning like this one?

I couldn't remember what I was wearing, so I peeked down at my T-shirt and realized the tag was tickling my neck. Sliding my arms out of the sleeves, I turned it around so the sunshine design was on the front. A backward shirt was something Mom would usually notice but . . . not today.

Everyone clapped and woo-hooed when Lisa Wu finished her song. She took a little bow. "We go to a club on Tuesday nights," she said. "Everyone loves to sing karaoke. Who wants to be next?"

I hoped Dad wasn't thinking now was a great time to show off his singing skills. Luckily, he just sat there with an amused look on his face.

Katherine was the first to volunteer. She sang a song in Chinese she'd learned at school, and she sang perfectly on-key, without sounding nervous at all.

Everyone cheered and asked her to sing another one. Which she did.

I was glad when we pulled up in front of an old brick two-story building and the karaoke came to an end. A hush fell over the van, and everyone stepped out and climbed the steps in silence.

"Why isn't anyone talking?" I whispered to my mom.

"Shhh," Mom said for an explanation.

The lady who greeted us at the door wore a long straight skirt, her dark hair pulled back tightly in a bun. She led us to a great big room with large windows, tile floors, and wooden benches lining the sides.

Then we waited and waited, without much talking. There was nothing interesting about the room, and the view out the window was gray skies and another ugly brick building next door. The families kept to themselves, and when I finally got to the point where I was ready to walk over to Katherine just to listen to her chatter, the ladies walked in with the babies.

The room filled with the hum of excitement. "Look, Emily! Here they come!" Dad said as the parade of babies passed by, each in the same pink jumpsuit except for one little boy, who was wearing blue.

"There she is! That's Mei Lin!" Mom said, pointing to the smallest in the bunch. One of the ladies called out, "Yiang, Mei Lin? Saunders family?"

My parents waved their arms in the air, and the woman made her way toward us. The cinnamon roll and yogurt and banana bread I'd eaten for breakfast sloshed together in my stomach in a funny way as the lady handed the baby, *my sister*, to my mom.

"Mei Lin," Mom said softly as she held her close. Tears filled her eyes again, like the night before. "It's you, at last."

"Hi, baby!" Dad said in this funny high-pitched voice, like he was talking to one of our cats. "It's your daddy!"

"Hi, Mei Lin," I said softly. I reached for her hand. She was tiny, same as in her photo. Long bangs covered her forehead and lots of dark shiny hair fell to her shoulders. "I'm your big sister, Emily."

Mei Lin didn't seem to notice I was talking to her. She was too busy squirming and looking all around the room. For the next few minutes, Mom dabbed at her eyes, Dad cooed, and I finally pulled out my digital camera, though I probably could have reached for Nana's and no one would have even noticed. I didn't plan to use the photos in the contest, but my parents were too taken in by Mei Lin to reach for theirs.

We spent a long time in the room filled with crying babies and toddlers, trying to get Mei Lin to pay attention to us instead of everything else around her. I handed her one toy after another, which she'd shake for a minute, then toss down on the floor.

"Do you want to hold her?" Dad asked me.

I shook my head. I'd never held a baby before, and she seemed content while Mom and Dad took turns holding her. Besides, I didn't want to risk the chance that she'd turn into one of the howlers in the room. "How much longer do we have to stay here?"

"I don't know," Mom said. "We have to wait until they call us for our paperwork."

Dad put a hand on my shoulder. "I told you it would be a long morning."

The minutes crept by. I put away my camera and tried not to get in the way while my parents held Mei Lin, fed her, changed her, and calmed her down whenever she started crying.

A little while later, I heard a squeak and looked up to see Katherine. She was walking around the room with a baby whose shoes squeaked every time she took a step.

They stopped in front of me. "Madison," Katherine said, "Can you say hello to Emily? *Ni-hao!*"

I waved at Madison, who was at least twice as big as Mei Lin and looked more like a little girl than a baby. Her parents had changed her out of the jumpsuit and into a sundress that matched Katherine's. She had an opening in her top lip so you could see her front teeth. "*Ni-hao*, Madison!"

Madison didn't answer. She just stood there, marching up and down to make her red shoes squeak.

"How old is she?" I asked Katherine.

"Twenty-three months." She looked over at Mei Lin, who was lying on her stomach on the blanket, kicking her feet and reaching for the strap on the diaper bag. "How old is Mei Lin? Doesn't she know how to walk yet?"

"Not yet," I said. "She's only eighteen months."

"Most babies walk by the time they're one," Katherine said. "Can she say any words yet?"

"Not that I've heard. She's pretty quiet."

"I was talking by the time I was eighteen months," Katherine said. "In full sentences."

"Everyone learns at their own pace," I said, quoting my dad. According to him, I didn't speak until I was two-and-a-half. *And you haven't stopped talking since,* he always said with a grin.

Katherine stared at Mei Lin. "But, doesn't she crawl or anything? Are you sure she's not a Waiting Child?"

"She crawled halfway across the room," I told her, even though I'd only seen her crawl a few steps before she flopped down on her belly. "Mom says she'll go straight from crawling to running. And we're the ones who've been waiting, not Mei Lin. We've waited over seven years."

Katherine's mouth dropped open and she clapped a hand over it. Then she said, "You should get her some squeaky shoes. Maybe that will help."

"Hey, Katherine," I said, wanting to ask her about her secret instead of worrying about whether something was wrong with Mei Lin. But Madison stomped her feet and tugged on Katherine's hand before I could get the words out. "Better go!" she said as Madison pulled her away. Hopefully there would be plenty of time to talk later. Hearing about a secret would certainly liven up things a bit and keep my mind off my own worries.

I turned to my mom. "When will Mei Lin learn to walk?"

"I don't know," Mom said as she filled a bottle with formula. "She'll get there soon enough."

I nodded. If Mom didn't know babies were supposed to walk by the time they were twelve months old, I wasn't about to tell her.

"Do you want to give her a bottle?" Mom asked.

"Okay." I sat down on the bench, and Mom put her in my arms.

"Be careful," Mom warned. Mei Lin was squirming all over the place. "You have to hold her tight."

"I'm not going to drop her," I said, tightening my arms around her. She let out a squeal. I tried to hold the bottle the way I saw some of the other parents doing, but she grabbed it out of my hands and fed herself.

Her eyes closed as she sucked away on the bottle. Did she even know who was holding her? Had she noticed me at all?

Mei Lin got heavier and heavier as she sat in my lap. I knew she didn't have any plans to move until she finished that bottle.

"Hey, you're pretty good at this," Dad said. "Where'd you learn to take care of babies?"

"I didn't," I said, handing Mei Lin back before he got any ideas about babysitting.

After hours of sitting inside a stuffy building with crying babies, the people in charge called us to sign some papers. Finally! Now we could do something fun.

"Well, we have twenty-four hours to decide if we want to keep Mei Lin," Dad said as we climbed back in the van.

"You mean . . . we can give her back?" I asked.

"That's how the Chinese government sees it. We don't sign the official adoption papers until tomorrow." Dad grinned. "So, what do you think?"

I didn't know what to say to that. I raised one eyebrow. "You're kidding, right?"

Mom put her arm around me. "Of course your dad's teasing! We have no plans to give your sister back. She's ours to keep."

I looked over at Mei Lin sitting in Mom's lap. She'd settled down for once, her eyes half-closed as she sucked on her fingers.

"I've got a great place we can go when we get back to the hotel," I told my mom.

"It might be a good idea for Mei Lin to have a nap."

Before I had a chance to say anything else, Lisa Wu spoke into the microphone again. "Next stop, Walmart!" she announced with a smile. "You can buy everything you need. Diapers, strollers, baby bottles, clothing. This is a good store to shop, like in America. You'll love it!"

CHAPTER SIX

I groaned. "Walmart? Can't we ask her to take us back to the hotel?"

"Shhhh," Mom said, putting her finger to her lips.

I crossed my arms in front of my chest and flopped back against the seat.

"I'm not crazy about Walmart either," Dad said.

"Then why do we have to go?"

"It's okay, Emily," Dad whispered. "I'm sure we won't be there for long."

Mom gave me a warning look, and I knew what it meant. But I didn't care if I was being rude. We had an entire foreign country to explore, and we were going to spend the afternoon in Walmart?

We pulled into the parking lot of a three-story building. Then we stepped inside. It was bright, flashy, and definitely the loudest Walmart I'd been to in my life. It was also packed with people, like we'd shown up for the Day After Christmas Sale or something.

We found a cart for Mei Lin, who was suddenly wide awake. She looked around like it was her first trip to the circus.

The other families put their babies into carts, waved at us, and disappeared right into the crowds. Mom and Dad stood there in the entrance looking even more lost than they had in the airport.

Well, I wasn't about to stand there all day. It was time for action. I grabbed onto Mei Lin's cart. "So, where to now?"

Dad shook his head, his hands over his ears. Booming music blasted from huge speakers and a high voice sang in Chinese. A disco ball like the one at the skating rink spun around and around shooting lights everywhere.

I glanced down at Mei Lin, afraid the loud noise and lights would make her burst into tears. But she gazed around, eyes wide open, taking it all in. So, I pushed her past the cashiers at the front, toward the escalators, where signs covered with Chinese writing had arrows pointing in different directions. "Should we go upstairs, or downstairs?"

"We need to find the baby section," Mom said, acting more like her regular self. "And maybe some groceries, too."

"Then let's go," I said.

"But, wait!" Mom rushed after me. "Shouldn't we ask someone first? We could wander around this store for hours."

"Good idea," Dad said. "There's someone in a Walmart vest over there." He pointed to a worker who stood in the middle of the electronics section. I pulled out my digital and snapped a few pictures. The place was crammed full of stuff. CDs and stereo equipment stood next to a display of lotions, perfumes, racks of chopsticks, and little bottles of liquor. I giggled when I spotted the red bras.

"I heard about this!" Mom said. "It's a lucky bra, since red is considered a lucky color."

I giggled some more. People squeezed past us as we made our way down the narrow aisle. I'd been dragged to a lot of Walmarts, but I'd never seen one quite like this.

Dad walked up to one of the workers. "Excuse me?" he yelled. "We're looking for the baby section?"

When the man shook his head, Mom pointed to Mei Lin. She cupped her hands over her mouth and yelled, "Baby stuff? For babies?"

The worker shrugged and pointed toward the middle of the store.

"I don't know if he understood us," Dad said, steering the cart away from the noise. "We'll try this way."

I snapped a few more shots and followed behind. "Hey! Squeaky shoes!" I said, spotting a display in the aisle. I ran over to pick up a blue pair. "Katherine said these will help Mei Lin learn to walk."

Dad laughed. "Since when did Katherine become an expert on babies? She just became a big sister today, same as you."

"Katherine's kind of an expert on everything," I said.

"More like she *thinks* she's an expert on everything—" Dad said but Mom hushed him.

"Madison was wearing a pair of squeaky shoes and she's a really good walker," I said. "Maybe it would help."

"She's almost two, a lot older than Mei Lin," Mom pointed out.

"But can't we get Mei Lin a pair?" I squeaked the shoes and Mei Lin reached for them.

Mom picked up a pair. "Look at the price. Fifteen yuan! That's only two dollars."

Dad nodded. "Well, you can't beat that deal. And once Mei Lin starts walking, at least we'll always know where she is."

So, we ended up buying two pairs of squeaky shoes for Mei Lin, and a pair of Pokemon flip-flops for me. I wasn't a fan of Pokemon, but it was either that or Hello Kitty. People in China must love Hello Kitty, because it was everywhere I looked—on shoes, towels, clocks, purses, pajamas, you-name-it.

The baby section was right around the corner. With all the stuff Mom and Dad had packed, I couldn't believe we needed a single extra thing. We ran into the Bresners, and guess what? They gave Mom and Dad a whole list of things we'd forgotten to bring.

The best part about running into the Bresners was that they already knew their way around the Walmart. It didn't hurt that Katherine could read the signs. After we filled our cart with baby stuff, Mr. Bresner said they needed groceries too so all of us took this escalator that had super wide steps for the carts and soon we arrived at the bottom level.

As we passed shelves full of breads and rolls, we landed in a section that really stunk. The smell of swamp water and something rotten almost made me gag and I plugged my nose right away.

All around us were bins heaped with food. Rice. Shrimp. Creepy-looking things with antennae, piled up high. A dead fish stared at me with an unblinking eye. I shivered.

"Dad, what's that?" I asked as we walked quickly past the open bins. I pointed to the big brown capes that hung from the low ceiling.

Dad looked up and squinted. "I think . . . they're dried bats."

"Bats! Why are they hanging from the ceiling?"

"I guess people eat them," Dad said. "They're a delicacy around here."

"You mean like insects?"

"Yup." Dad gave me a playful punch on the arm. "Look at it this way, Em. People from China think a lot of our food is weird too. Like tongue, or chopped liver, or pickled pigs' feet, to name a few."

"Yuck." I made a face, but I was already reaching for my camera. This was what someone might call an Attention-Grabber, and if I did it right, it could turn out artistic, even if it was a dead bat. "I don't eat any of those things," I told my dad.

"Well, not everyone in China eats bats or insects either."

I figured Dad had a point, but after I snapped a few photos, I grabbed hold of the cart and pushed it out of that section quick as I could. I flew right past the turtles, frogs, and crocodiles—all ALIVE—that had somehow ended up in the food section instead of the pet section.

"There's the *real* food aisle," Katherine said with a giggle as she pointed straight ahead. I picked up speed and followed her, finally taking in a breath of fresh air. Now here were some things we could actually use!

I grinned at Katherine, and we began picking up items like peanut butter, crackers, and chips, tossing them into our carts. "So . . . I'm really good at keeping secrets," I told her, thinking it was the perfect time for her to spill.

Katherine nodded. "That's what I thought." Her eyes sparkled, and she leaned closer to me. Then she whispered. "My parents don't know it, but while I'm in China, I'm going to find my birthmom."

CHAPTER SEVEN

My mouth dropped open, but she just smiled and nodded again.

"Hey, what's going on here?" Dad said, taking a look at the items I'd thrown in our cart. I was still staring at Katherine, wanting to hear more about her plans. Mom had told me the law was complicated. The government limited the number of children a family could have, so babies were left at the orphanage because parents couldn't take care of them. But, it was also against the law for anyone to give up their babies, so when the orphanage found them, they didn't know who the parents were. How in the world was Katherine going to find her birth-mom if the *orphanage* didn't even know who she was?

Mrs. Bresner's sharp voice snapped me out of my thoughts. "What did I tell you about junk food, Katherine?" She reached for the groceries and started stacking them back on the shelves. "This is your chance to visit your homeland, to sample real Chinese cuisine."

Katherine groaned and rolled her eyes, but she looked over at me and winked. Now that she'd shared a secret, it felt like we were on the same side. Something close to friends, even.

Mrs. Bresner was too busy restocking the shelves to notice the eye-rolling and the look that passed between us. My parents didn't notice either, as they were too busy checking out the items I'd stashed in the cart. Luckily, they must have already been having cravings for familiar junk food because they didn't return a single thing.

I was standing at check-out in the longest line ever, still thinking about what Katherine had told me, when I felt someone pull on my ponytail. I turned around, thinking it was my dad. Instead I saw a pretty lady with long dark hair, and she was smiling at me.

Then she held up her camera and pointed it right at me.

I shook my head and took a step backward, but Dad smiled back at the lady. He turned to me and lowered his voice. Not that it mattered. She probably didn't understand a word he was saying. "We should have warned you," Dad said, squeezing my shoulder. "Lisa Wu told us that people might want our photos since they don't see Americans around here very often, especially ones with curly red hair like yours."

Oh! I remembered the lady who chased me to the elevator and pulled my ponytail when I was exploring on my own. *So that's what it was all about?*

I swallowed. "But I don't want my picture taken. She can take Mei Lin's." I looked down at Mei Lin, sitting quietly in the cart, her brown eyes gazing out from underneath her long bangs at all the sights around her. She didn't weigh much, and she hadn't made a sound the whole time we were in the store, almost as if she were in a trance. The Super Walmart in Changsha trance, which could definitely be a thing.

"She wants *your* picture, Emily," Dad said. "Come on, honey. Be a good sport. It'll only take a second."

I let out a big, loud sigh. But I gave in and posed while the lady took the photo.

"*Xie-xie,*" the lady said before she pushed her cart away.

"It's weird," I said after she walked away. "Why would she want a picture of me?" "Because you're beautiful," Mom said.

I made a face.

"It's true. Besides, you stand out in the crowd. How many girls have you seen around here with red curls and freckles?"

"It's rude to stare," I said.

Dad laughed. "She wasn't staring. She wanted a photo, that's all."

I rolled my eyes. If you don't want a stranger taking your picture, then you should be able to say no. This was the second time it had happened, and even though Dad thought it was funny, I didn't like it at all.

Next time we left the hotel room, I would put my hair up under a cap.

By the time we made it back to the room, Mei Lin was sound asleep. So far, she seemed like a pretty good baby. Mom put her down in the crib and she didn't even wake up while we ate a perfectly yummy lunch—peanut butter on crackers, chips, and soda.

'To stop thinking about Katherine and her secret plans, I pulled out my list of tourist attractions. If I didn't make some plans of my own, we'd end up wasting another afternoon. "We could go to the Provincial Museum," I told my parents. "That's the one the Bresners went to yesterday."

"Mei Lin needs a good nap," Mom said, glancing over at the crib. "She is worn out, and I can tell you from experience, babies are no fun when they're exhausted."

"She can nap in the stroller," I said, glad we'd picked one up at Walmart. "Babies do it all the time."

"We have paperwork we need to finish up, too," Mom said.

How much paperwork could one baby possibly need? "I bet the Bresners aren't going to stick around the hotel room all day doing boring paperwork."

Dad glanced at his watch. "Actually, it's almost three o'clock. I don't know if we can squeeze in a trip to the museum—"

"How about a trip to Orange Lake then?" I studied my travel guide. "It says you take the Number 4 bus and it's all very quick and easy."

"What's at Orange Lake?" Dad asked.

"Orange trees," I said. "Lots of them. And a big lake, and a temple, and you can go hiking."

"Let me see," Dad said, reaching for my guide. "Hmmm, this looks really interesting. Great research, Emily!"

"Dan, we are not chasing after buses today," Mom said firmly. "I'm sure it's not as quick and easy as it sounds. And didn't you hear what Lisa said? Buses aren't supposed to be great for tourists."

Dad paused a minute then snapped his fingers. "Hey, I just remembered something else we forgot to buy at Walmart."

"What?" I asked.

"One of those baby backpacks, so we can go on hikes with your sister."

"We could take the stroller," I said. "I'm sure there are some paved paths."

"This is Mei Lin's first day with us," Mom said. "It's been stressful and tiring for her, and I'm not about to make it worse by taking her to a place where she's even more uncomfortable."

Dad paused a minute then dropped his head and nodded. "You're right, Lynn," he said. Then he turned to me. "We'll have plenty of time for exploring China. We're here for two whole weeks, you know."

"Lisa has a lot planned for us in the itinerary," Mom said. "She's going to keep us busy enough and we'll be able to ride in the van with someone who actually knows the area."

"But what about today?" I asked. "We're not going to do anything the rest of the afternoon?"

"Mei Lin's going to take a nap and we're going to finish our paperwork," Mom said very slowly and clearly. I knew that tone. It was the *'Because I said so'* tone, and I knew there was no point in fighting it.

I let out a big sigh and flopped back down on the bed.

"Emily." Mom said my name in a way that told me she wouldn't keep her patience for long.

"Tell you what," Dad said. "After Mei Lin's nap, we'll explore the hotel. Check out some of the shops. Maybe go bowling?"

I sat up. "Okay," I said, remembering the shop with the little glass balls.

"And for dinner we're all meeting in the playroom," Mom said. "Guess what we're having tonight?"

"Grilled bats' wings?" Dad teased.

"Pizza," Mom said. "They have a Pizza Hut close by."

I smiled. But just for a second. Pizza Hut sounded much better than having to tackle chopsticks at another Chinese restaurant, but it was something we could eat any time. Exploring Orange Lake was not something we could do at home. Would we ever visit a really cool place during this trip, where I could take awesome pictures? Or were we going to spend the whole time in old brick buildings, Walmarts, and hanging out in our tiny hotel room?

If I wanted to win the contest, I was going to need more than a photo of a dead bat hanging from the ceiling, even if the picture was taken clear across the world in China.

***

While Mei Lin napped and Mom and Dad did paperwork, I plugged in my laptop and typed in: How to find your birthmom in China.

A number of articles popped up. Some girls had found not only their moms, but dads, sisters, grandparents, and cousins.

I glanced over at Mei Lin, snoozing away in a little pink dress we picked up at Walmart. I studied the way her chest rose and fell with each breath, her almond-shaped eyes, her tiny feet and hands, her perfect red lips. I was officially a big sister, but so far, Mei Lin seemed like a fragile little doll. She had no idea we were her new family.

Right now, she was caught between a family she didn't know in China and a family she didn't know in the United

States. But she wouldn't be a little doll forever. Eventually she'd get to know her new mom and dad, the way Katherine had, and her new sister, too.

And someday, like Katherine, she might wonder about the family she left behind.

I snapped the laptop shut. It was all too complicated, and it made my head spin. Besides, I was in China to find my own adventure and to win a contest, not to help Katherine find her birth family.

A little while later, Mom and Dad finished their paperwork, which didn't turn out to take as long as they had predicted. They could have put it off until that evening and I bet we could have fit in that trip to Orange Lake after all, with Mei Lin sleeping soundly in the stroller. She was still out cold an hour after we got back, so what do you know? My parents decided to take advantage of the peace and quiet and nap along with her.

"Thirty minutes," Dad said, "and then we'll explore the hotel."

I didn't even bother to protest this time around. I needed to stop thinking about Katherine's secret and look for my own adventures. So, I waited until they dozed off. Then, I pulled my hair up under a cap, dropped Dad's cell phone and room key into my backpack, and slipped out of the room without even writing a note. I knew from recent experience that once they fell asleep, it would take a pretty loud noise to wake them.

Running down the hallway to the elevator, I planned my outing in my mind. First stop: the bowling alley on the bottom floor. Lisa had told us it was at the end of the hall, so I ran in that direction, figuring I'd hear the sounds of crashing pins before I arrived, but I almost walked right past it.

The room was small, with three lanes and a snack bar, and the only person I saw was a man behind the bar, drying glasses. I hesitated in the doorway a minute. I wanted to play, but if we came back another time, my parents might find out I'd been sneaking around.

The man looked up. "*Ni hao,*" he said, waving at me.

Which made me feel a little braver. If he didn't speak English, he wouldn't be able to tell my parents anything, so I tried another question to be sure. "How much does it cost?" I asked.

He shook his head and pointed me to a lane. Which meant I was safe to play, and it wouldn't cost a thing. I got started right away, the sound of the bowling ball and the clatter of pins echoing in the room. It was pretty basic as far as bowling alleys go, no barriers to keep the ball from hitting the gutter, pencil and paper to keep score instead of a computer screen.

Thankfully my score wasn't posted on the wall or up on a screen; without the barriers, I hit a lot of gutters. The ball always started out straight, then about halfway down the alley it would make a sharp turn to the left or right, and *Clunk*! Into the alley it would go.

If Dad were standing next to me, he'd be full of pointers. It was kind of fun being in the bowling alley all by myself with no one watching or telling me how to do things. And then, on my eighth frame, something amazing happened.

I knocked down all the pins with one roll.

"Score!" I cheered, jumping up and down as the machine cleared the pins from the lane. I didn't realize I'd yelled out loud until I heard clapping coming from the bar. The worker stood there, clapping and grinning. "I can't believe it!" I said, and then I curtsied.

A few minutes later, still floating from my victory as I waved goodbye to the man at the bowling alley, I glanced down at Dad's cell. I'd been gone for twenty-five minutes!

I raced down the hallway, trying to decide if I should take the elevator or the stairs. Luckily the elevator was on the ground floor, so I hopped on, crossing my fingers that everyone was still asleep in the room. That's when I realized I hadn't taken a single photo on my outing, and while it had been fun bowling a game and hitting a strike, hanging around a hotel was not exactly going to help me win the contest. And my adventure may have been about to land me in a heap of trouble.

When the elevator opened, I raced down the hall. Taking a deep breath, I leaned my head against the door of our room, listening for sounds. Nothing. Whew! I turned the key as quietly as I could and stepped inside to find the room exactly the way I'd left it.

Except for one thing. Mei Lin was standing up in her crib, staring right at me.

CHAPTER EIGHT

I dropped my backpack on a chair, and after a quick glance to make sure my parents were snoozing away, I turned to Mei Lin.

"Hey, little girl, what are you up to?"

Her brown eyes stayed glued to mine. I reached for the polka-dotted elephant in the crib and held it up. "Hello, Mei Lin!" I said in a high voice as I wiggled the elephant. "My name's Polky! Do you like to dance?"

Mei Lin let out a squeal. Then she reached for Polky and tossed him on the floor.

"Hey, don't throw me!" I said, picking the elephant back up. This went on for a while, with Mei Lin squealing and throwing the stuffed animal and me picking it back up. She was playing a game, but when I heard Dad's cell phone ring from inside my backpack, I jumped.

I turned to get the phone, and Mei Lin howled, loud enough to wake my parents from their nap. Dad sat straight up in bed. "What? What is it?" he yelled.

I shrugged. "Your phone rang," I said, handing it to him, "and Mei Lin started crying."

Mom jumped out of bed and went to pick up Mei Lin, and that made her cry even more.

"What's wrong with her?" I asked.

"Nothing's wrong," Dad said. "She's just exercising her lungs, that's all."

"Shhhhh, shhhhh," Mom said as she paced back and forth with Mei Lin.

She sure could hit the high notes. I clamped my hands over my ears. When Dad stepped out in the hallway to listen to his message, I stepped out with him, eager to get away from the noise. "The families are meeting at five o'clock in the playroom," Lisa was saying. "See you there!"

Dad glanced at his watch, then at me. "Looks like we won't have time for bowling this afternoon."

I shrugged. "That's okay." I knew if I protested and Dad changed his mind, there was a good chance we'd run into the same worker, and even if he didn't speak English, he'd make it clear he remembered me after my amazing strike.

"Sorry, Em," Dad said, giving my shoulder a squeeze. "But after dinner, we'll do some exploring, I promise."

"You mean it?"

Dad nodded. "If Mei Lin's too tired, Mom can take her back to the room and we'll spend a little time together, okay?"

"Okay." I could still hear Mei Lin wailing inside the room. "Can I go to the playroom and wait for Katherine?"

Dad hesitated. I never expected to beg for time with Katherine, but I was curious about her plans even if I wasn't sure I wanted to help. Besides, whatever she had to say would be way more interesting than sitting in a small hotel room listening to Mei Lin cry.

"Hey, what's with the cap?" Dad asked, pulling it off my head.

The cap! I'd forgotten to take it off when I walked back into the room. "Just felt like wearing it, that's all," I said, trying to sound casual about it. He examined me as I raked my fingers through my curls. My dad wasn't that observant, was he? Surely he wouldn't put it all together, that I'd put my hair up so no one would take photos of me *while I was out exploring the hotel?* Before he could think about it too much, I repeated my question. "So, is it all right if I go to the playroom to meet Katherine?"

Dad hesitated a few more seconds while I held my breath. Then, he handed me the cell phone. I couldn't believe it! Dad was trusting me in China to go somewhere on my own? "We'll be there in a few minutes. If you need to get in touch with us, call Mom's cell. And don't go anywhere besides the playroom, understand?"

"Got it," I said, trying not to grin too big as I reached for the cell. Even if he was only letting me go down the hall, it was a first step worth celebrating.

***

The playroom was full of toys and had a cushioned bench beneath windows that covered the entire wall. Katherine wasn't there yet so I pulled out Nana's camera and snapped some photos of Changsha's skyline.

Mei Lin had calmed down by the time my parents wheeled her down the hall in her new stroller. As soon as Mei Lin was lifted out of her stroller, she crawled right over to a walker. It looked like a big yellow tire on wheels. She put her hand on the walker and let out a happy shout.

"I think she wants to try it out," Mom said.

Dad picked her up and put her in the seat in the middle. She began paddling her feet. "Wow, look at her go!" Dad said.

I took off after her. Mei Lin paddled out the doorway, with me close behind. Mom and Dad stood in the doorway to the playroom and watched as she stopped in front of the elevators. I turned her around to push her back to the playroom.

"Emily!" Katherine called to me as she walked up the hall with her family. They were the last from our group to arrive. "How did Mei Lin get all the way over here?"

"She walked. Come on, Mei Lin. Let's go play with Madison in the playroom."

But Mei Lin didn't want to go back in the playroom. All she wanted to do was walk on the carpet outside the elevators. Katherine's parents stood at the playroom door with Mom and Dad as Mei Lin paddled the walker back and forth, Madison running along beside her.

"Hey, I bet she had a walker like that at the orphanage," Katherine said. "Mom said they tie it to the wall with a rope so they can't go far."

"I guess that's a good idea." I imagined a whole group taking off in walkers, the orphanage ladies running after them.

"So, what did you do this afternoon?" Katherine asked as we followed the babies down the hall. Before I had a chance to answer she said, "We spent the afternoon at the Provincial Museum, since we didn't see all of it yesterday." She let out a big sigh.

I looked over at her. "I thought you said it was a great museum."

"It was. But there's lots to see in China. I don't have to read every single plaque about China's history, the way Mom wants me to. And besides, Madison was cranky, and let me tell you, visiting a museum with a fussy baby is no fun at all. We should have come back so she could take a nap, and then I could have at least gone swimming or something."

"Oh. Well, that's what we did. I mean, I didn't get to go swimming, but Mei Lin took a long nap while Mom and Dad were doing paperwork . . ." I hesitated, wondering if I should tell her about sneaking off on my own. I was dying to tell someone, so the words popped right out. "Then Mom and Dad took a nap, and I went bowling."

"By yourself?"

I nodded. "I rolled a strike, too."

"Really? My parents won't let me wander around the hotel by myself. They've been sticking to me like glue this whole trip so far."

"Yeah, well, my parents didn't let me either," I said. "But once they were asleep, I went anyway."

Katherine's eyes widened. "I knew it! I knew you'd be good at sneaking around. That's why you'll be perfect for helping me with my plan. Promise you won't tell?"

I avoided her eyes, afraid to make a promise I might not be able to keep. "If it were me, I'd tell my parents. It seems like a big thing to try to do on your own."

Katherine crossed her arms in front of her chest. "Mom and Dad don't want me to look for my birthmom."

"Why not?"

"Mom said it could lead to disappointment. That we might not be able to find her, or that she might not want to see me. But, even if I don't find my birthmom, I could find my dad, or my sister. Mom wants me to wait until I'm older, but I'm here in China right now, and it might be harder to find her if I wait. So . . ." She grabbed me by the wrist and locked eyes with mine. "Are you in, or not?"

I bit my lip, but I could see the hope in her eyes and I could hear it in her voice. That's when I remembered the photojournalist contest, the one I was determined to win. I'd memorized the directions, which I recited in my head: Tell a story with photos and words. Your goal is to effectively combine photography and writing to make a powerful statement about your topic.

If I wanted to tell a powerful story, the perfect one had just dropped in my lap.

I looked over at Katherine and nodded. "Okay," I said. "I'll help. And I promise not to tell."

CHAPTER NINE

We reached the end of the hall. Mei Lin banged her walker right into someone's hotel room door. "Come on, Mei Lin." I turned her around before she could bang the door again. "Let's go back to the playroom to see Mommy and Daddy."

Mei Lin moved her feet, paddling that walker right back down the hall.

Katherine squeezed my hand, then let go. "Thanks."

"Anytime," I said. I was so excited I'd figured out how to win the contest that I could hardly keep from jumping up and down. "So, how are you going to find her?"

"I'm going to put up a letter at my finding spot, and I'll leave my cell phone number." She held up a little pink phone.

"Your finding spot?"

Katherine nodded. As we came around the corner, Madison ran into the playroom, right past the Bresners, who were standing with my parents waiting for us in the doorway.

"Hey, wait for me!" Katherine called after her. "You know what? Madison is really smart," she said to me. "She can count to ten in Mandarin. Come here, Madison!"

Katherine tried to pick up Madison, but she stomped her squeaky feet and shook her head.

"Come on, Madison. Can you say your numbers for Emily?"

Madison stomped her squeaky feet again and yelled, "NO!" Which I guess is the same in any language. Then she grabbed a toy off the shelf and started pushing the buttons.

"I guess she'd rather play than count," I said.

Katherine rolled her eyes. "I told you she's been grouchy today."

"So, what did you mean by finding spot?" I asked, but before she could answer, my parents burst in.

"There you are, Mei Lin!" Mom cooed. "We were wondering where you disappeared to."

"Did you see her go?" I said. "She took off down the hall and we could hardly keep up with her."

"Mei Lin, you must be exhausted." Mom lifted her out of the walker.

Mei Lin let out a shriek. And it wasn't a happy one. So, Mom decided to let her stay in the walker a little bit longer.

***

I didn't have a chance to speak with Katherine alone again for the rest of the evening. There were always adults hovering around, and the babies sure made a racket. I was dying to hear more details of Katherine's plan and find out exactly how she expected me to help, but I figured it would have to wait until the next day.

Pizza Hut pizza in China was the best ever. The crust had just the right amount of crunch and the cheese stretched in a yummy way every time I took a bite. Best of all, we got to eat with our hands instead of chopsticks. After we ate, we wandered in and out of the shops until they closed, just like Dad promised.

When we walked into the store with the glass balls, the man looked right at me and gave me a big smile. "You're back!" he said.

Mom wasn't paying attention because she was busy with Mei Lin, but Dad raised his eyebrows at me. "What does he mean, you're back?"

"Nothing." I shook my head quickly. "He's mixed up, that's all." And then I pretended like I'd never seen the little glass balls before. "This is so cool!"

I could feel Dad's eyes on me long enough to tell me he was suspicious. But as soon as he noticed the man writing inside the balls, he became amazed instead.

We ended up buying one with a whale on it for me and a giant panda for Mei Lin, and the artist printed our names in Chinese characters and our birthdays on each, which was really cool.

Dad stopped me as we walked away. "Emily . . . are you sure there's not something you need to tell us? Did you come down here this afternoon instead of going straight to the playroom?"

I shook my head again, but I couldn't look him in the eye.

Luckily, Mom came to my rescue. "Dan, she asked us to trust her, and that's what we should do."

Dad paused a minute. Then he said, "I guess you're right. Sorry about that, Em." He brushed the top of my head with his hand.

I let out a slow, quiet breath. Good thing Mom and Dad didn't know how completely out of it they were when they napped.

The rest of the evening was great. Even though I'd been to some of the stores on my own, it was fun exploring with my parents, and everyone was in a good mood, even Mei Lin. While I hadn't seen Mei Lin break out in a smile or laughter, Katherine's sister seemed way grouchier, especially the way she always had a frown on her face. When we headed back to the hotel room, Mei Lin fell right asleep.

Mom and Dad fell asleep right away, too, but I tossed and turned all night, imagining all the fantastic photos I was going to take so I could wow the judges in the contest.

CHAPTER TEN

China, DAY 3, 4/5/14
Dear Diary,
I am officially a Big Sister! Mei Lin seems like a
pretty good baby so far. All the others in the
group were wailing away while we wasted half the
day in some boring government building waiting to
sign paperwork. I couldn't really blame them. Mei
Lin seemed okay about it though.

Today she woke up at FIVE in the morning,
ready to start her day! So that meant the rest
of us had to get up before dawn too! The only
good thing about that was we were first in line
for the breakfast buffet.

Mom asked for steamed egg for Mei Lin, which
looked like a bowl of vanilla pudding. She gobbled
it right up, then grabbed my banana bread. So
Mom gave her some of that, and some toast and

melon, too. For a little thing, she sure can eat!

We are on our way back to the government building today, to make the adoption official, according to Dad. It seems like anyone who goes to all the trouble of filling out tons of paperwork and having a social worker visit the house and planning a trip to China would already have their mind made up. But maybe some people take one look at their child and decide they don't want to be parents after all.

That definitely isn't what happened in my family. Mom and Dad took one look at Mei Lin and their hearts melted.

I'm a photographer, so it's something I noticed. And you know what?

Even though I'm not crazy about babies, the first time I saw Mei Lin, my heart melted just a teeny bit, too.

Love,

Emily

(hopefully off on a better adventure

than to Walmart)

The van was waiting for us at nine o'clock. Katherine waved as we sat down behind them. "Madison cried all night," she said in a droopy kind of voice. Today her hair hung straight down her back without any fancy braids, but I noticed she wasn't too tired to pick out a short skirt with a matching top.

"Mei Lin woke us up at 4:47 a.m."

"Madison fell asleep at midnight. And woke up at three." Katherine yawned and pulled a granola bar out of her bag. "Then she went back to sleep. And she slept so late that we missed breakfast."

"We went to breakfast." I yawned too. "Because we were all awake before the restaurant opened."

It turned out to be another morning that stretched on and on. A lady showed us to the same large room where we'd waited for Mei Lin the day before. I almost curled up on the bench and went back to sleep.

"What's wrong with her?" I asked when Mei Lin started crying for the fourth time. "Yesterday she hardly cried at all."

"Looks like she's getting a cold." Mom wiped Mei Lin's nose. "I don't think she feels too well."

"Maybe she ate too much," I said. "You shouldn't have fed her so much if she'd never had solid food before."

Mom shook her head. "No, I don't think that's the problem," she said but I took a few steps away, just to be safe. I definitely did not want baby puke all over me. Mom rocked Mei Lin to get her to stop crying. I tried to get Mei Lin to smile. I tried my funniest silly faces, and I used my best voices to put on a show with her toys, but she just pushed me away.

Mei Lin was grouchy, and she wasn't the only one. The room was full of other crying babies who were tired of waiting.

I was starting to feel a little grouchy, too. I shook out my arms and legs to try to wake up. I glanced over to the other side of the room where Katherine's family seemed to be going through the same thing. This seemed like the perfect time to find out more about finding spots and how Katherine planned to get in touch with her birthmom. "Can I push Mei Lin around in the stroller?"

"I think I better hold her for a while. Can you hand me the pink blanket in the baby bag?"

I searched through the bag and in the zipper pockets along the side. I didn't see a pink blanket. "I think you forgot to pack it."

Mom sighed. "Emily, I asked you to pack it. Remember, I said that I'd put the blanket in Mei Lin's crib?"

I shook my head. I didn't remember Mom saying anything about a blanket. "Why do you need the blanket? I thought you wanted to hold her."

"It might make her feel better. I think she needs a nap. She went to sleep so easily with the soft blanket last night."

Big sigh, from me this time. It wasn't my fault Mei Lin had been crying so loud I didn't even hear Mom ask me to pack the blanket.

"When are they going to call us to go in the other room?" I asked a few minutes later.

"Hush, hush," Mom said to Mei Lin, who was still crying.

"And what are we going to do in there?" I asked. "Didn't you already fill out all the paperwork?"

"One thing you can count on around here," Dad said, "is there's always more paperwork."

"But why?" I asked. "If you already signed the papers, why do you have to keep signing them?"

"Shhh shhh shhh," Mom was saying to Mei Lin.

"Remember when we told you today's the day we have to make it official?" Dad said.

I nodded. "But still. Couldn't we just sign the papers at the hotel? Lisa could bring the papers here and we wouldn't have to waste our time. Then we could take Mei Lin back to the hotel for her nap, and she would stop crying. Did you ask Lisa if she could have brought the papers for us"—"

"Emily." Mom stopped hushing for a minute. Her voice was firm and sharp, like pins and needles. "Of course we had to come here today. If we want to bring Mei Lin home, we have to follow all of the rules. Now can you please stop asking so many questions? I am trying to get Mei Lin to quiet down."

Well! I sunk down onto a chair. All I was trying to do was help. I pulled out a fantasy book I'd brought with me and moved over to the bench along the wall. Taking care of a new baby was for the birds. I tried to concentrate on my book, but my mind was racing. I tried to recapture my excited feelings about the contest from the night before but all I could think about was the way Mom had snapped at me.

Finally, after a hundred hours, Mei Lin stopped crying. When I looked over at her, she was sound asleep on Mom's shoulder.

Mom sat down next to me. She smiled and patted my hand. She leaned back on the bench and closed her eyes. I put my book down and closed my eyes, too. I almost dozed off, right in my chair.

A little while later, a lady called us back into an office. Mei Lin stayed asleep while Mom and Dad signed papers. Then they had to answer a lot of questions. Mei Lin snoozed away. Next, they dipped her feet into red ink to make a footprint for her birth certificate. Mei Lin slept right through it.

When we went to another room for the photo, Mei Lin opened her eyes. She yawned and looked around, but she didn't cry.

"Now we need one picture of the Saunders family for adoption record," the lady told us.

I ran my fingers through my hair. My ponytail was coming loose. Mom didn't like it when hair covered my face, so I tucked a few strands behind my ears and hoped that I looked neat enough for a family photo. Then I followed my parents to the front of the room.

The lady taking the picture shook her head. "No, no, we only need three in adoption photo. You," she said to me, "come over here and wait until I take picture."

I couldn't believe it. I felt like a moldy zucchini from the back of our refrigerator. I looked over at my parents. Didn't the lady know that *I* was part of the family, too? I waited for Mom and Dad to correct the photographer.

Dad gave my ponytail a tug. "It's okay, Emily. It's just another of those regulations. It'll only take a minute."

I walked over to the side of the room and sat down quietly. I watched as Mom and Dad leaned in close together, holding Mei Lin between them. My parents smiled big smiles. They looked like one big happy family. They seemed to have forgotten that something was missing.

Me.

CHAPTER ELEVEN

It was noon by the time the van clunked its way back to the Dolton. But after a quick lunch in our room, we headed out on a group tour of a silk museum. It wasn't my top choice of Exciting Things to Do in China, but it was better than sitting around a hotel room. Besides, I figured it would give me a chance to talk to Katherine. A million questions bumped around inside my head and I couldn't wait to find some answers.

We walked quietly through the museum as Lisa Wu acted as tour guide, translating the plaques and telling me more than I ever wanted to know about the silk worm and how it spins silk. The best part of the tour was the huge paintings covering the walls of the museum. If you stood up close, you could see the detailed scenes were actually made of silk threads.

Unfortunately, there was no time for private conversations as we followed Lisa around and listened to long explanations. Mei Lin slept on Mom's shoulder through all of it but some of the other babies let us know how bored they were with a lot of squawking whenever we stopped to listen to Lisa's speeches.

When we finally finished the tour, we ended up at the silk shop next door where everything you could imagine was made from silk. Clothes, pillows, mattresses, toys, you name it! The whole room was full of stuff and most of the parents in the adoption group, except for mine, seemed ready to spend a lot of money. So we stayed in the shop for a long time.

"I'm going to talk to Katherine," I said, spotting the perfect opportunity to get away from my parents.

"Take Mei Lin," Mom said quickly, strapping her back into the stroller.

I found Katherine with her parents, looking at the quilts. When she saw me, she grinned. "Madison and I are going to walk around for a while," she told her parents as she unbuckled Madison from her stroller. The Bresners didn't try to stop her, even though there was a lot of stuff a toddler could get into. They were probably as glad for a break as mine were.

"What'd you think?" Katherine asked as we walked around the shop.

"The paintings were kind of cool," I said. "But I was getting a little tired of hearing about the silkworms."

Katherine nodded. "That's for sure."

"So . . . I've been dying to hear more about the plan!" I told her, the words rushing out of me. "What are finding spots? When are we going to post the letter, and how are you going to do it without your parents or mine finding out? And, what are you going to do if your birthmom contacts you?"

"*When*," Katherine corrected me. "Not *if*."

"Okay, when." I took a deep breath. "So tell me about the finding spots."

"Well, it's against the law for parents to abandon their babies," Katherine said. "No, Madison, you can't have that!" Madison had grabbed an embroidered silk pillow and had stuck it in her mouth. Katherine put the pillow back on the table and Madison started to shriek.

"Let's go look at the stuffed animals," I suggested. "I saw some around here somewhere."

Katherine grabbed Madison's hand and pulled her over to another display that didn't look as expensive. "Here," she said, handing Madison a stuffed monkey. "You can play with this." But Madison didn't want the monkey. For the next few minutes, we tried out an assortment of animals until we found a tiger. She finally stopped shrieking, and then Mei Lin started, her little arms reaching out from the stroller.

"You were saying?" I asked when they both settled down, a silk stuffed animal in both of their arms.

"Parents leave their babies in places where they know they'll be picked up and brought to the orphanage. The officials take a photo of the baby and they print it in the newspaper."

"Why? Anyone who leaves their baby is giving it up for adoption, right?"

"I guess." Katherine's eyes clouded over for a moment. "It's not the mom's fault, though. China has really strict laws about how many babies you can have."

I nodded. I still didn't understand how the whole thing worked. The government didn't let you keep your baby, but it was against the law to give the baby up? How did that make any sense at all?

"So, my birth family probably lives near my finding spot. So, if I tack up a letter, chances are someone will see it. If not my birthmom, then another friend or relative at least."

I bit my lip. I understood what Katherine was saying, but according to what I learned in math class this year, the *probability* of it actually happening would be pretty low. In a city of millions, Katherine's birth family, if they still lived nearby, would have to walk by the finding spot during the exact time Katherine was in China. And since we were already on our third day of the trip, we didn't have many days to spare.

In other words, the odds of Katherine finding her birth family AND my chances of winning the photojournalist contest with a story of a reunion were about one in a million.

"I've already written the letter," Katherine said, in a voice that sounded dreamy.

"But . . . how do you even know where your finding spot is?"

"The adoption guide told my parents. They'll show us Madison and Mei Lin's too while we're here—hey, Madison, wait up!"

Madison had taken off around a bamboo screen. That's when we heard a loud clatter. Katherine and I stared at each other with wide eyes then raced after Madison to see what damage and destruction she had caused.

CHAPTER TWELVE

Oh no!" Katherine gasped when we spotted the rack of clothing on the floor, silky dresses and blouses on hangers strewn all over the place. Madison sat in the middle of the wreckage, banging a hanger on the tiles and squealing with joy.

"No, Madison!" Katherine said, trying to scoop her up. "Bad girl!" Madison just squirmed out of her arms and squealed some more.

The Bresners rushed over. "What happened?" Mrs. Bresner asked, her cheeks flushed.

Katherine shook her head. "Madison wouldn't listen to me. She just took off, and then she pulled down the whole clothing rack!"

"You shouldn't have let her out of your sight," Mrs. Bresner said while she reached for Madison.

"It wasn't my fault. I tried to stop her, but she was too fast."

Mrs. Bresner didn't respond to Katherine, just began picking things up and hanging them back on the rack. A saleslady appeared around then and tried to tell Mrs. Bresner not to worry. First, she said something in Chinese, then gave us a quick smile. "It's okay. We fix it."

Mrs. Bresner kept apologizing while Katherine just stood there, not saying anything. I was glad when her dad put an arm around her and said, "Don't worry about it, honey. Luckily, she didn't break anything."

I wished Mrs. Bresner would say something nice, or at least smile at Katherine. She's the one who let Katherine walk off with Madison without telling her to use the stroller. But Mrs. Bresner stayed focused on cleaning up the mess instead of worrying about how Katherine felt.

I wanted to finish our conversation, but it was clear it wasn't going to happen right then. "I'm going to find my parents," I told her. She nodded without looking back at me.

***

Once we got back to the hotel, my parents put Mei Lin down for a nap.

"Tell you what," Dad said to me, "we're going to run over to Lisa's room for a little while to ask her some questions—"

"Questions about what?" I glanced over at tiny Mei Lin snoozing away in her crib. I thought about the way Madison had run all over the store that morning while Mei Lin was content to sit in a stroller. "Mei Lin's okay, isn't she?"

Dad scrunched up his eyebrows. "What do you mean?"

"You know," I said, looking down at the floor. "That she's not walking yet, and she hardly even crawls."

"There's nothing wrong with your sister," Mom said. "She just needs some time to catch up."

Mom sounded like she believed what she was saying, so I just shrugged. "What are you going to Lisa's for then?"

"The group is visiting the orphanage tomorrow," Dad said. "We're trying to decide if we want to go."

"Hey, I've got an idea!" I said, snapping my fingers. "We could go to Orange Lake instead! It would be so much more fun than visiting a boring old orphanage. Mei Lin will love it!"

My parents exchanged looks, but I had no idea what they were thinking.

"We haven't seen any of the pretty parts of China yet," I pointed out. An idea was forming in my head, an alternative to the "Girl Finds Birthmom" story, just in case it didn't work out. "Besides, the orphanage means another day stuck inside."

"We'll see what Lisa has to say about it," Dad said. "Orange Lake does sound like a nice place to visit, doesn't it, Lynn?"

"Sure," Mom said, but I could tell she was seriously considering the orphanage. "We'll see, okay, Emily?"

"We'll be back in a little while," Dad said. "Keep an eye on Mei Lin."

"Got it," I said, crossing my fingers they'd decide against the group tour.

After they left the room, I pulled out my journal and flipped back to My Fears About the China Trip. So far, I was making progress. I'd already checked off the fear of flying and eating authentic food, and I moved my finger down to #5: *What if I don't like Katherine and I'm stuck hanging out with her for two weeks?* I smiled and checked that one off, too. Katherine and I were different, but she was beginning to grow on me. Besides, she'd pulled me into an exciting adventure, and if things worked out the way she hoped, I'd win the contest for sure.

And if they didn't? Well, I already had a back-up plan.

I plugged in my laptop and opened the contest document. Then I typed

```
Plan A: "The Reunion in China: Adopted
         Chinese Girl Finds Her Birthmom"
Plan B: "The Beauty of China in Expected
         and Unexpected Places."
```

Mei Lin stirred in her crib and her little elephant jingled and fell to the floor. She let out a cry. She was just like me, needing her stuffed animal to fall asleep! So I picked up the elephant and tucked it in next to her, straightening the pink blanket so she was all comfy. She sighed softly, rolled over, and went back to sleep.

I sat back down at my computer, thinking about the next day. A trip to Orange Lake with its temples and waterfalls and orange trees would give me some expected beauty. But the photo of a bat hanging in Walmart might work for the rest of the title, and the more I looked at the country and its people I was sure to find other things that would surprise me.

While I was hoping for Plan A, a back-up plan wouldn't hurt.

A knock on the door shook me out of my thoughts. I shut my laptop and jumped up to see who was there.

"You want to go swimming?" Katherine asked when I opened the door. I could see a purple bikini through her cover-up. "Dad's taking me while Madison naps."

"Really? No Provincial Museum today?" I teased.

Katherine rolled her eyes. "Thank goodness, no. Madison's stunt today wore Mom out. She doesn't like it when her children misbehave."

I laughed. "Madison's just a baby."

"Yeah, and I was the one in charge." She shrugged. "Oh well. So, are you up for it?"

"Mom and Dad went to Lisa's to talk to her about something. But if you wait for me, I'm sure they'll let me go."

"Okay." Katherine grinned and waved at me. "See you in a bit!"

I changed into my bathing suit while I waited for my parents, packing Nana's camera along with my towel. We were only allowed fifteen photos for the contest, but you had to take a lot to get the right one. The pool was the perfect place to capture Katherine's spirit. I could bet she was an expert swimmer, just like she seemed to be an expert at everything else. If I could get a photo of her diving into the pool it could have a bigger meaning than the obvious one.

Like Nana always said, *"Let your photos dig beneath the surface. Look for the extraordinary in the ordinary."*

That's exactly what I was going to have to do if I wanted to win the contest.

After my parents returned, I rushed off to Katherine's. They said they needed some time to discuss the trip tomorrow, so it worked out perfectly.

Katherine was an awesome swimmer, just as I had predicted. Our voices echoed inside the room and bounced off the walls, so we didn't have a chance for private conversation at first, but when Mr. Bresner decided to swim some laps, I took advantage of the opportunity.

"So, when are we going to put up the letter?" I whispered to her. "We're leaving Changsha at the end of the week!"

"Come on," Katherine said. "Don't you think I'm a better planner than that? I was born in Guangzhou, and we'll be there for seven days!"

"Good," I said. "I was afraid we were running out of time."

"Don't worry," Katherine said. "We can look at Lisa's itinerary for next week. I'm sure there's some free time when we first arrive."

"But how are we going to sneak out without our parents finding out? They keep a pretty close eye on us, you know."

"Simple. I tell my parents I'm with you, and you tell your parents you're with me, and we sneak out when they're too busy to pay attention to details. With a new baby, it shouldn't be too tricky. My parents seem a bit overwhelmed, how about yours?"

I grinned. It could definitely work.

"Hey, let's see who can get the rings!" Katherine said, tossing them into the water. I dove in after her. Meeting Katherine in China had turned out better than I ever imagined. I couldn't believe that just a few days ago I thought we could never be friends.

***

"Aren't the rest of the families coming?" I asked that evening as we headed out to a new restaurant down the street.

Dad shook his head. "I guess Lisa figured we've had enough togetherness over the last few days. She said tonight we're on our own."

"But—but don't we need a translator?" I asked. Even though I'd spent most of the day with Katherine, I wasn't sure about ordering at a restaurant where the menu was in a different language.

Dad laughed. "Lisa wrote something that will help." He held up a piece of paper with symbols all over it.

"What does it say?"

Dad peered at it closely as if he could read it. "It says 'Do not feed this family snake, insects, or duck. *Especially* not the duck.'"

I giggled.

"Don't worry," Mom said. "We'll get a good dinner tonight, I promise."

I wasn't so sure about that, but I remembered #2 on my List of Fears. I'd already checked it off, which meant I'd conquered my fear of real Chinese cuisine. So I squared my shoulders, held my chin high, and followed my parents into the restaurant with red awnings and a name I couldn't read, hoping my parents were right.

CHAPTER THIRTEEN

Heading out for dinner on our own turned out to be a total disaster. I should have guessed it would be from the moment I saw the gigantic tank full of lobsters in the front lobby. It was a loud, bright place where voices echoed off the high ceilings and wooden floors, and I could barely hear my parents, who were sitting right next to me.

The waiter brought a high chair for Mei Lin without a tray, which meant she had a grand old time grabbing everything she could on our crowded little table.

"Wheeeeeee!!!" Mei Lin squealed, reaching for the china spoon. She immediately dropped it on the floor, and it smashed into a million pieces.

Things got worse from there. Dad showed the waiter Lisa's notes, and the waiter asked a few questions in Chinese that of course we couldn't understand, then walked away, shaking his head and muttering.

While we waited for our food, I spent the entire time picking up chopsticks and napkins Mei Lin kept tossing on the floor. It was a little like that game with Polky the elephant but definitely not as fun.

When our dishes arrived, I had no idea what was what. There was a bowl of green slimy stuff that must have been some kind of vegetable, another plate that might have had burned tofu on it, noodles coated in a dark brown sauce so you couldn't see the vegetables or meat that might have been hiding underneath, and of course, white rice without soy sauce. I was ready to send it all back, but I'd already checked #2 off on my List of Fears.

So I started with the tofu. Since Lisa wasn't around, I speared a chunk with a chopstick and stuck it in my mouth. Aargh!!! My mouth was on fire! Since I couldn't spit the food out, I forced myself to swallow it down before reaching for my glass of water to wash out the bad taste.

"What's wrong?" Dad asked me.

I waved my hand in front of my mouth. "Spicy! Don't let Mei Lin eat it!" I said, but when I looked over at Mei Lin, she was slurping it down like cottage cheese.

"Looks like she loves it," Mom said. "Try another bite, Em. Maybe it's not so bad."

I shook my head, picking at the rice on my plate. At least Mei Lin hadn't broken all the spoons, so there was something I could manage to eat.

"Try the Chinese broccoli," Mom said, pointing to a green blob that looked like overcooked spinach.

"That's okay," I said, shaking my head again.

"Here." Mom scooped some of her food onto my plate. "It's noodles and shrimp."

It looked just as gross as the rest of the food at the table. Had I really checked off #2 on my list of fears? The dishes at the hotel didn't look anything like the ones in front of me. I pushed my chair back from the table and held up my hands. "Forget it. I'm not eating THAT."

Mei Lin grabbed a noodle and tossed it. It landed right in my hair. "Stop it, Mei Lin," I snapped at her.

"Emily," Mom warned.

"Sorry," I mumbled. I was trying to have a good attitude and I really wanted to be an adventurous, daring person like Nana. But it was hard when you were hungry and everything on the table looked, well, DISGUSTING. I was sitting there dreaming about real Chinese food, the kind we got at Wang Fu's at home, when Mei Lin reached for my water glass.

"AAIIIEEE!!" she cried out.

I jumped out of my seat as the flood of cold water splashed across the seaweedy broccoli and onto my lap. "Mei Lin!" I yelled at her. "Look what you've done!"

Mei Lin burst into tears. This time when she started shrieking, it was louder than ever before.

While I took a napkin and tried to dry up some of the water that had splashed all over my clothes, Dad stood up from the table. "Well, I guess this brings this dinner to an official end."

***

"Look at it this way," Dad said as he opened the hotel carry-out container full of French fries and onion rings, "You win some, you lose some."

"I sure am glad Mei Lin decided to spill the water," I said, reaching for an onion ring. "We'd still be stuck at the worst restaurant ever if it weren't for her."

"I wouldn't say the worst restaurant *ever*," Dad said. "How about that one we stopped in on the way home from Florida?"

"We'd been driving for hours and couldn't find a place to stop—" Mom said.

"And everyone was getting so cranky!" I said, jumping right in. "And when we went inside it was crowded and everyone was drinking these great big drinks with little umbrellas and the food was really gross!"

"We were so hungry we ate it anyway," Mom said with a laugh. "And we didn't notice the sanitation sign until we walked out. It was a 72! The lowest rating I'd ever seen."

We started talking about all the bad restaurant experiences we'd had, and by the time we'd finished off the hotel junk food, I'd decided there were plenty of awful restaurants back in the states, too.

"So, what are we doing tomorrow?" I asked as Mom got Mei Lin ready for bed. "Can we go to Orange Lake?"

"We've decided to go on the trip to the orphanage after all," Mom said.

"Oh." Disappointment shot through me. "Mei Lin would like Orange Lake much better."

"Maybe. But this is an important trip, both for us and Mei Lin."

I didn't bother to ask why, but I didn't argue with them either. "Is everyone else in the group going?" I asked.

Mom nodded. "So you'll have Katherine to talk to. You two have hit it off, haven't you?"

"She's really nice," I said. *And sneaky,* I thought to myself. For a moment, I wished I could tell my parents about Katherine's plan to find her birthmom. There was so much about adopting a baby from China that I still didn't understand and keeping secrets from Mom and Dad made me feel a little funny inside. But there was no turning back now. I'd made a promise and Katherine was counting on me.

I finished off the last onion ring and threw the container in the trashcan. "We're not going to be there all day, are we?"

"It's a long drive out in the country," Dad said. "So it might be a long day. Better get a good night's sleep."

As it turns out, I was more tired than I thought. All of us went to bed a little while later, and I only read for a few minutes before my eyes started to close. I fell fast asleep.

It seemed like I'd just dozed off when Mei Lin's screams woke me.

Mom flicked on the light and jumped out of bed. "Mei Lin's warm," she said, her voice on edge. "Do you know where the thermometer is, Dan?"

Dad rolled out of bed and searched for the thermometer. I sat up and rubbed my eyes, glancing at the clock. *2:31.* "Is she okay?" I mumbled.

"We'll see," Mom said as she tried to quiet Mei Lin down. "Go back to sleep, Emily."

I closed my eyes, but I could hear my parents' worried voices. Next thing I knew, Mei Lin was throwing up formula all over Mom, then Dad. And then she started to howl even louder.

I sat back up again. "What's wrong with her?"

"She's all right," Dad said in a tired voice as he cleaned up Mei Lin. "Babies throw up sometimes."

"Did you find the thermometer?" I asked.

"She has a low-grade fever, only 101," Mom said as she rocked her.

But what if her temperature goes up? What if she has the stomach flu and gets really sick? I thought to myself but didn't ask out loud. Mom and Dad seemed like they had things under control and I didn't need to make things worse by asking a bunch of questions.

I rolled over and tried to go back to sleep even though my head filled with worries. After a while, the room became quiet again. Dad yawned and climbed back into bed. Mom gave Mei Lin some medicine and put her back in the crib then turned off the light. I listened for Mei Lin's steady breathing until I finally fell back asleep.

Mei Lin slept until almost eight, and so did the rest of us. When she woke up, she wasn't crying, just lying in the bed making baby sounds. Her fever was gone, and she drank up the bottle Mom gave her. I watched her carefully from a distance to see if she was going to puke afterward. When she didn't, Mom and Dad decided it was safe to go on the trip to the orphanage.

"We gave her some medicine and I'll pack towels just in case," Dad said to me with a wink.

"I'll get her pink baby blanket," I said.

"Thanks, Emily." Mom let out a long breath as we headed downstairs for breakfast. "I'm just glad the fever's gone."

"Me too," I said, and Mom squeezed my hand.

CHAPTER FOURTEEN

China, DAY 4, 4/6/14

Dear Diary,

I'm worried about Mei Lin. She woke up in the middle of the night with a fever and she threw up all over the place. I had a hard time going back to sleep even after she settled down. What would happen if she got really sick and had to go to the hospital? How could we help her if we couldn't understand what the doctors were saying?

Here's something else I'm worried about: Mei Lin is so tiny and maybe she's not strong enough to fight off infections. She only weighs SIXTEEN AND A HALF pounds, which is the size of a seven-month-old, not the size of an eighteen-month-old. I know because I looked it up just now and that's what I found out and it's the truth.

This morning her fever's gone, and Mom and

Dad seem to think it was just a cold and she'll be okay. I never thought about it before, but it must be tough to be a parent and try not to worry about all the things that could go wrong with your baby.

Well we're off to the orphanage today! I was hoping we'd skip the trip because it sounds like another boring day. How will I ever find any good photos for Plan B of the contest if we spend all our time in government buildings?

Love,
Emily
(whose sister is hopefully not sick anymore)

An hour later, we were on our way to the orphanage. Mom still had a concerned look in her eyes, but Mei Lin seemed fine except for a few sniffles as she leaned back against Mom, sucking her fingers.

It was a long drive. We left the city, and soon we drove out into the country, surrounded by nothing but green fields and rice paddies. After a while, Mei Lin fell asleep, and Mom wasn't far behind.

Katherine turned around from the seat in front of us. "Do you want to sit with me, Emily? Over there?" She pointed to an empty pair of seats across the aisle.

"Sure!" I said, jumping up quickly. There were too many parents close by to discuss our Guangzhou plans so Katherine and I talked about normal stuff like school and friends and hobbies. I even decided to tell her about the photojournalist contest, though I didn't tell her that "Girl Finds Birthmom" was a topic that might give me the winning entry.

"I like to take pictures, too," Katherine said, "but I'm not that good at it. Mom says I'm too much in a rush to snap the picture."

"Well," I told her, "That's one thing Nana taught me. You have to be super patient."

"That would be great if you won," Katherine said. "I've never been to New York."

"We go to the city a lot. You just take the train and the subway and you're there in an hour and a half," I said.

"Lucky," Katherine said.

"But the camp is at a college, so we get to spend the week in a real dormitory," I said.

"Cool," Katherine said. "Will you let me see your project when you're done? Even if you don't win, it will be really special to have all those photos of when you first met Mei Lin."

"My project's not about Mei Lin," I told her. "The judges don't want to see a bunch of pictures of a baby."

"But it's not just a baby," Katherine said. "It's your *sister*. You're supposed to tell a story in the contest, right?"

I nodded.

"Getting a baby sister is an important story, don't you think?"

I shrugged and glanced over at Mei Lin, asleep in Mom's arms. "I'm thinking I'll take photos showing China's beauty," I said. "Unexpected and expected."

"Well, that's up to you. But I think you're missing out on a winning entry. Hey, guess what I like to do for fun?"

"What?" I asked her. I knew she was a great swimmer, and Mrs. Bresner had bragged about how she'd been playing violin since she was four and had been on a gymnastics team since second grade.

"Fix people's hair," Katherine said with a grin. "I could French braid your hair if you want."

"Really?" I looked over at the long twisty braid that hung over one shoulder. "You do your own hair?"

"Sure! Someday I want to have my own salon. Katherine's Creations. What do you think?"

"I love it!" I said.

"Mom doesn't. She thinks fashion and hair styling are a waste." She lowered her voice and leaned in closer to me. "'With your brains, you can write your own ticket. You can be a doctor, lawyer, whatever you dream of!'" Katherine frowned.

I nodded, totally getting what she was saying. "Mom and Dad think I should be an engineer someday since I'm good at math. But I want to be a photojournalist. That's why I want to win the contest—to show my parents I'm serious about it."

"Then you should take my advice," Katherine said with a grin. "Tell the adoption story. The judges will love it."

I shrugged. "We'll see," I said, my stomach flipping. I didn't tell Katherine that's what I hoped to do, only I'd be telling her story instead of Mei Lin's. *Technically I'm not lying*, I tried to convince myself. *I just told her Plan B instead of Plan A.*

"So, you want me to braid your hair? It will look great, I promise."

"Sure," I said.

***

An hour and a half after we left Changsha, we arrived at the orphanage in YiYiang City. I kept running my hand over the back of my head where Katherine expertly braided my hair. I couldn't wait to get to a mirror, so I could take a better look.

A security guard opened the iron gate for us. I stared at the two stone lions sitting on both sides of the entranceway until a woman greeted us at the door. "Welcome to YiYiang Orphanage," she said. "Today we will give you a tour and meet in the reception room afterwards. Is everyone ready?"

Everyone nodded and followed her down the hallway. Daycares are usually noisy places, so I expected to hear the chatter of little kids, laughter, shouts and squeals. In the background, I thought I'd hear music like you'd hear in most preschools. Instead, this place was strangely quiet, except for the sound of some babies crying.

"First we will go to a room where the infants are sleeping." The guide put her finger to her lips and opened the door to a small room with ten cribs lined up across it. None of the babies were actually asleep. Some were wiggling around, and one was crying.

The cribs were little and close to the floor. My heart skipped a beat. The babies were strapped to the railing. I tugged on Mom's hand. "Why are they strapped in?" I whispered.

"I guess they're afraid the babies might fall out," Mom said in a quiet voice.

Chills moved up and down my arms. Mei Lin had slept here, strapped into a crib when she was only a few days old. When she cried out in the middle of the night, did anyone come?

I glanced over at Katherine. She stood close to her mother, hugging herself with her arms, her mouth in a straight line.

The guide took us to the toddler room next, where the older babies slept. She opened the door to show us a room full of cribs in neat rows, all with straps. I counted quickly—six rows of six cribs each, mostly empty except for a thin blanket.

In my baby pictures, I had a shiny white crib with a soft colorful blanket. An assortment of stuffed animals, even though PuddleDuck was the one I loved best. A musical bunny mobile spun around above my head.

Mei Lin let out a cry. I looked over at her. She had turned her head away from the cribs, rubbing her face back and forth against Mom's shoulder. Mom reached for a tissue to wipe her nose.

"She's okay," Mom whispered to me. "Just a little sniffly."

"Everyone is playing now," the guide continued. "I will show you the playroom where they have fun," she said, moving us out of the room quickly.

The playroom was full of babies and young children. I started counting but it was hard to keep track. I spotted a few girls with cleft palates, like Madison, a little boy with hearing aids and another with thick glasses. Mei Lin stopped fussing as soon as we entered. There were only two ladies trying to keep an eye on all of them. One sat in a chair rocking a smaller baby who was crying.

When they saw us standing in the doorway, the room filled with squeals and excitement.

"She wants you to play!" the guide said when a baby crawled right over to me and tried to pull up on my legs.

In the meantime, Mei Lin had spotted the walker, attached to the wall with a strong rope, just like Katherine had said. This must have been where she spent a lot of her time. She struggled to get out of Mom's arms, but the tour guide wouldn't let us stay, which made Mei Lin start fussing again.

"We have to go," I said to the baby whose hand was on my knee. I tore my eyes away from her, and all the others who'd spotted us and wanted our attention.

We followed the guide to a clean room where everyone ate, stocked with high chairs, and after that she showed us the room for baths where they used a big sink for a tub. The tour didn't last long, and I knew the guide had only shown us a small part of the orphanage.

"What's down there?" I asked as we walked right past a long hallway.

"That's where the older children stay," she said. "Come, it is time for refreshments."

Older children. The word echoed in my head. Older meant they didn't get adopted when they were babies. Almost everyone wanted babies or young children, not eight or nine or ten-year-olds. That's when the truth hit me.

If they weren't adopted when they were little, they grew up in the orphanage, without a family of their own. I knew they were the ones on the Waiting Children list, children who might never find a home.

As we followed the guide to the room with refreshments, I looked over at Mei Lin in her red dress. She had quieted down by then, and when Mom fed her bananas and cookies, she ate them right up. We'd brought gifts for the orphanage staff—a box of chocolates, a red envelope with money in it, and a bag of clothes and toys for the orphanage.

We were finishing up our snacks when Mei Lin let out a loud shriek. All of a sudden, she was squirming in Dad's arms and shrieking away.

"Looks like Mei Lin recognizes her nannies," Lisa said, pointing to some of the orphanage staff who had entered the room.

Mei Lin reached her arms out in the direction of the ladies.

"Do you want to go see the nannies?" Lisa asked Mei Lin. From her cries, it was clear she did. One of the ladies broke into a huge smile when she saw Mei Lin and started talking away in Chinese.

"She says this is her special baby," Lisa explained. "That Mei Lin used to get jealous when Nano held anyone else. She wants to know if she can hold her."

Mei Lin squirmed to get out of Dad's arms. He handed her over, and she stopped crying. Nano spoke to her in a quiet voice, rocking her in her arms.

Nano held her for a long time, until it was time to go. Then she handed her back to Mom. Mei Lin started hollering again, reaching for Nano. As we walked out of the orphanage, Mei Lin was crying like I'd never seen before.

My stomach sloshed in a funny way. As we left the building where she'd spent the first eighteen months of her life, I stayed close by her side.

CHAPTER FIFTEEN

Mei Lin didn't stop wailing, even after the van started moving. Mom held her and rubbed her back, then passed her to Dad to try to calm her down. I sank down into the seat next to them. What had my parents been thinking, bringing Mei Lin back to the orphanage? Mom said she wasn't feeling well because of her cold, but she didn't start fussing until she saw the cribs. Had she been worried we would leave her there? After she saw Nano, was she confused about where she belonged?

I closed my eyes, trying to get the pictures out of my mind: the nursery lined up with back-to-back cribs and the playroom overflowing with babies and toddlers wanting our attention. Then there were the rooms we didn't see full of children in wheelchairs, or with Down syndrome, children who might have been missing a limb, or had heart trouble, or were born with other problems that weren't as easy to cure as a cleft palate.

As I thought about those rooms filled with children waiting for a home, I wished I'd never made the trip to orphanage. The images of what I'd seen would be etched into my mind, forever.

Mei Lin's jagged sobs pulled me away from the orphanage and back to where I sat in the van. I took a deep breath, her cries cutting right through me. Finally, I tried something that I hoped would work. I pulled out my camera, trying to distract her. "Mei Lin," I said, "Look over here."

My instinct had been right; Mei Lin was fascinated. The howls turned into quiet whimpers, and finally they just stopped. I took a video of the two of us, then I played it back. Mei Lin's eyes opened wide, and she reached for the camera.

"No, you can't have it, silly," I told her. "Someday, when you get bigger, you can be a photographer just like me."

Mei Lin took her hand away from the camera and reached for my hair instead.

"No, Mei Lin!" I said with a giggle as I unwrapped her hand from my thick braid. "Katherine worked very hard on that. Let's make another video, okay?"

"Good thinking, Emily," Dad said with a grin, and Mom patted my knee and smiled. I kept taking pictures and videos, and it worked like magic. It made Mei Lin forget about the trip to the orphanage, and it seemed to make Mom and Dad forget, too.

"I think I'm catching whatever Mei Lin has," Mom said a little while later when she sneezed for about the hundredth time.

"Come to think of it," Dad said, "My throat's feeling a little sore."

"I hope I'm not getting sick, too," I said, sniffling just to be sure.

"You'll be fine," Dad said. "We'll all feel better with a little rest."

By the time we pulled up in front of the hotel, Mei Lin's eyes were starting to close. Mom gave her some medicine as soon as we got to our room and put her right to bed. Then Mom took some medicine and went to bed, too.

Dad yawned and said, "Guess I better join them. Mei Lin had us up half the night."

I didn't protest, like I usually did. Part of me wished my parents would say something about what we'd just seen, and the other part of me wanted to try to forget about it altogether. The trip had worn everyone out, including me. I pulled out my book, trying to stop thinking about the way Mei Lin had sobbed when she had to leave her nanny.

The words danced around on the page and all I could see was the look of heartbreak in Mei Lin's eyes.

A few minutes later, there was a knock on the door. I dropped my book on the table and jumped up to answer it.

Katherine stood in the hallway, grinning at me. "Hey, do you want to go to the gift shops downstairs? Mom and Dad said we could go if it's all right with your parents. And look!" She held up a cell phone. "If there's an emergency I can reach my parents any time."

I peeked back into the room. There was no movement on any of the beds.

"Why don't you leave a note for them?" Katherine whispered. "I'm sure it will be fine." Katherine didn't have to ask more than once. *I'm getting pretty good at this*, I thought, as I tore out a piece of paper and scribbled:

Mom and Dad,
    I'm at Katherine's. Here's their cell phone number if you need me.
                                                Love, Emily

I grabbed my backpack and closed the door quietly behind me. "Just practicing for when we get to Guangzhou," I told her.

"Awesome!" Katherine said, giving me a high five. "So, I've been thinking, the perfect day to post the letter is next Monday."

I counted quickly. Today was Wednesday, which meant we were going to carry out our plan in FIVE days. "But will we have enough time to figure everything out?"

"Sure," Katherine said with confidence. "We fly to Guangzhou Saturday morning. It's only a ninety-minute flight, so we'll have half the day on Saturday and all of Sunday to explore Guangzhou with our families. Monday morning we go to the embassy, but we'll have the afternoon to ourselves. That's when we sneak out and put up the notes. We're here until Saturday so that gives my birthmom the rest of the week to get in touch with me. What do you think?"

"Sounds good to me," I said. "But how are we going to get to your finding spot? And what if it's really far from the hotel?"

"I've already figured that out. It's only 2.7 miles away. We could walk to the bus station and catch the Number 9 bus that will stop close by. Or, we can take a taxi. Mom and Dad gave me some spending money, and it shouldn't cost too much."

"Wow," I said as I followed her into a gift shop. "Where is your finding spot, anyway?"

"It's in a park."

"Really? She just left you in the middle of a park?" As soon as the words slipped out of my mouth I wanted to take them back.

"It's a finding spot," Katherine said sharply. "It's one of the places where the orphanage picks up babies. It's better than an old movie theater, anyway."

My mouth dropped open and I clapped it shut. Moms were leaving babies at abandoned movie theaters? "So," I said, trying to change the subject, "what did you think of the orphanage?"

Katherine paused as she ran her fingers over a tea set. "I don't really feel like talking about it, Emily."

I swallowed. If I had purposely picked the wrong question to ask, I couldn't have done a better job. If the trip had bothered me, I couldn't imagine how it must have made Katherine feel.

For the next few minutes we wandered around the shop in silence.

"That's pretty," I finally said when Katherine fingered a turquoise dress made of embroidered fabric. There were stacks of them on a table in plastic bags.

"I think I'll try it on. Mom said I could pick one out for myself and one for Madison. She turned to me. "You could buy a qipao, too, for the red sofa photos."

When I gave her a puzzled look, she said, "In Guangzhou there's this red sofa at The White Swan. That's where everyone always takes pictures of the babies and their families. We have a picture of me and my adoption group on the red sofa when I was eleven months old."

The lady who worked in the shop walked over to us and smiled. She was young, with blonde streaks woven into wavy hair that hung to her shoulders. She wore jeans, very high heels, long dangling earrings, and lots of gold bracelets. "Can I help you? Need try on?"

"Do you have a turquoise one, in my size?" Katherine asked.

"You like the dress or pants?"

"Dress."

"No problem. How about you?" she asked me, but I shook my head.

"Green would look good on you," Katherine said. "You should try one on."

I shook my head again, so the lady handed a qipao to Katherine and she disappeared into the dressing room.

A couple of minutes later, Katherine stepped out in her turquoise outfit. "You look beautiful," I told her, reaching for Nana's camera.

"Thanks. Hey," she said her eyes lighting up. "Am I one of the Unexpected Beauties for the contest?"

"Could be," I said with a grin, happy that things were back to normal between us. As she stood there admiring herself in the mirror, her cell phone rang. "If it's my parents, tell them we'll be back in a second!" I said quickly.

Katherine reached for the phone. "Hello? Oh, hello, Mr. Saunders. Yes, she's right here," she said, handing it to me before disappearing back into the changing room.

"Hi, Emily," Dad said. "You scared us for a minute there. Sure am glad you left a note."

"You were sleeping," I said. "I didn't want to wake you up."

There was a pause, like Dad was trying to figure out if he should give me a lecture about leaving when he was asleep. But then he said, "Yeah, I guess that makes sense. Well, we're getting ready to take your sister to the playroom. We'll meet you at the Bresners', okay?"

"Um, they're still resting," I said quickly. "We'll meet you at the playroom, all right, Dad?"

"Sure," Dad said.

"See you in a few. Bye!" I said, hanging up before Dad changed his mind. "Come on," I said when Katherine came out of the dressing room, breaking into a run. "We better take the steps. And don't say a word about the shops—"

"Being sneaky is so much fun!" Katherine said. "Don't worry, I've got you covered."

CHAPTER SIXTEEN

CHINA, DAY 5, 4/7/14

Dear Diary,

The orphanage was hard. Hard for me, hard for
Mei Lin, and hard for Katherine. It's one of those
things I'd never thought about before. I knew Mei
Lin was in an orphanage because she didn't have
parents to take care of her, but I never thought
about what it meant until I saw it with my own eyes.

Now I wish we had never gone.

Luckily Mei Lin has forgotten all about it-she's
only eighteen months old, after all! And luckily,
her fever didn't come back, and no more puking
either. She still has a stuffy nose which looks
a little gross, but all the babies here have colds.
Mom says it's because they're being introduced
to new germs. So, I guess that means she'll catch
everything that comes along for a while. Fun, fun!

Also, there's been something on my mind
for a while that I haven't shared with you. The
good news is I have the perfect topic for the
photojournalist contest. Hooray! Here's the short
title: Adopted Girl Finds Birthmom in China.

The bad news is I've agreed to help Katherine,
who's the subject of my project entry. That
means a lot of lying and a lot of sneaking around.
And while I'm excited about the adventure, I've
never kept something big like this from my
parents before.

And then there's that other lie, the one that's
wearing a hole in the pit of my stomach. I haven't
told Katherine the truth about the contest.
Yet. I mean, I plan to tell her about it before I
send in the photos, and I'm sure she won't care
because by then I would have helped her find her
birthmom and that's all that will matter ... but still.
Something about what I'm doing feels very wrong.

We're heading to the Pearl Market today, which
sounds a lot better than some old brick building!

Love,
Emily (whose sister likes cameras a lot too!)

Over the next couple of days, Lisa Wu kept us busy with lots
of shopping. We went to all kinds of gift shops with more
art, clothes, furnishings, and tea sets. My favorite place was
the Pearl Market, a two-story mall full of bead shops. You
could find any kind of bead you wanted, in every shape and
in a rainbow of colors, but everyone was most interested in

the pearl necklaces. That's because pearls are really expensive everywhere but China.

"Aren't you getting one for Mei Lin?" Katherine asked as I sat beside her while she strung a necklace for Madison. "Mom made a pearl necklace and bracelet for me when I was a baby. Only I'll have to wait until I'm eighteen—it's the tradition."

I shrugged. "I don't think she's planning on it. Eighteen's a long time to wait for a gift."

Katherine wrinkled up her nose. "I know. But you should do it. Mei Lin would really like it."

I looked over at Mei Lin in her stroller, reaching for a necklace. I giggled. "You're probably right. I'll go talk to Mom."

A few hours later, we walked out of the shops with a pearl necklace for Mei Lin and a bracelet for me with blue beads the color of the ocean. Luckily, I didn't have to wait until I was eighteen to wear mine.

On Friday, our last day in Changsha, Lisa said we were going to spend some time exploring the city. We visited a park along the river that had tons of old statues and big trees with thick branches covered with moss. It didn't look so different from a park you might see in the United States, except for the people.

A bride in a floofy white dress and big sunhat was getting her picture taken. I spotted a few couples who were ballroom dancing in the middle of the square, a jambox booming out old-fashioned music. Then we passed a large group gathered to exercise together, but they were doing it without making a sound. They stood with their arms and legs in different positions, like balancing on one foot with their hands on their hips.

"It's called *Tai-ji*," Lisa explained as we watched the group move in slow motion to another position, raising a hand above their heads and sticking one leg straight out in front of them. "It's a form of meditation."

It was sort of like yoga, but a lot more interesting. Plus, no one was giving commands like "Downward Facing Dog!" or "Sun Salutation, now breathe . . ."

The people looked a lot like the stone statues in the park, except they were alive. I reached for my camera and started snapping pictures.

We watched the Tai Chi people for a long time, and then we walked on the paved trail circling the lake. Mom pushed Mei Lin in the stroller while Katherine and I ran ahead. This time I was able to pull out Nana's camera to take some great photos of Katherine as she stood on the bridge overlooking the lake. I about jumped right out of my skin when someone tapped me on my shoulder. Had my parents suddenly picked up speed on their stroll, and caught me in the act?

An older gentleman held up his camera and smiled at me. I quickly slipped Nana's camera back in the bag.

Katherine's mouth dropped open. "He wants to take your photo! He thinks you're someone famous!" she squealed.

"It's the hair," I said, twisting a curl around one finger. Katherine just giggled and leaned in close to me as he snapped the photo.

"Two for the price of one," she joked. The old man nodded his thanks and walked away. "Come on!" I grabbed Katherine's hand and took off down the trail before anyone else got the same idea.

After the park, Lisa Wu took us on a tour of Changsha. We drove through the downtown, where big skyscrapers stood next to little shops selling meat on a stick. I bet they sold fried bugs, too, but I decided to keep that to myself.

A man stood in the middle of the street on a little platform. He was holding an umbrella, even though it wasn't raining, directing traffic. Horns honked and lots of cars swerved in and out of lanes and it was all very exciting.

"Okay. Now it is time to see the finding spots for your babies," Lisa Wu said after we'd been driving around for a while. That's when it got really quiet in the van. Katherine turned around in her seat and gave me a knowing look.

"It's where the moms left their babies," Dad explained to me since he had no idea I already knew all about it. "They picked places where they knew people from the orphanage would be looking for them."

"Why didn't they just bring her to the orphanage?" I asked.

Dad shook his head. "It's the way things are done. Shhh, listen," he said as the van pulled up in front of a social welfare building and Lisa started calling out names.

The building was old with moss growing over it. It reminded me of one of those creepy orphanages you see in movies, even though it wasn't an orphanage at all. I held my breath, hoping she wouldn't say Mei Lin's name.

Luckily, she didn't, and a few minutes later we pulled up in front of another park with big shady trees. "This is the finding spot for Mei Lin and Sylvie," Lisa announced.

I clamped a hand over my mouth.

I stared out at the park, trying to imagine it. She'd been just a tiny baby, only a few days old. What if it had started to rain? Goosebumps raised up on my arms. I ran my hands over them, as if suddenly it was the middle of winter instead of a warm muggy day. She might have only been a few days old, but she had to know she was being left behind.

How long did Mei Lin cry as she waited for someone to find her?

"How old was she?" I whispered to Mom.

"They think she was five days old."

"So, they don't know for sure? They don't know when her real birthday is?"

"They estimated. It's probably close enough"—"

"But how could her mother just *leave* her there?"

Mom put her arm around me. "I'm sure it wasn't easy . . . but she couldn't keep her baby."

"Did someone tell her to leave her at the park? How did she know what to do?"

Mom looked over at me, her eyes shining. "The mothers in China know about the orphanages and how they work," she said quietly. "They don't feel like they have a choice, Em. But they know the babies will find good homes."

In just a few days, I'd help Katherine put up a note at her finding spot. Staring out at a tree with thick mossy branches, I thought about the mom who had to leave her baby behind. I hoped with all my heart that Katherine's birthmom would have a chance to see that her baby had turned out just fine, and to learn that Katherine loved her birthmom even though she'd given her up.

My eyes flickered to Mei Lin, asleep in my mom's lap. The van started moving again, driving toward the places the other babies had been left. Tears filled my eyes. I reached out to hold Mei Lin's hand. Mei Lin's fingers curled on top of mine, holding on tight.

CHAPTER SEVENTEEN

GUANGZHOU, CHINA, Day 7, 4/9/14
Dear Diary,
Today we flew to Guangzhou on a teeny tiny
plane. Our hotel is called the White Swan, and it is
fantastic!
   There have been a lot of changes in a week.
I've become a world traveler, a big sister, and I've
made a new friend.

I stopped and twirled my hair around my finger. All these
things were great, but my heart was weighed down with worries, new ones to replace the ones I'd written down before leaving for our trip.

   I've been doing a lot of lying lately, and I don't
feel too good about that.

I checked off the list in my head: Lying to my parents about Nana's camera, lying to my parents when I'd been sneaking out of the hotel room while they were sleeping, not telling Katherine the truth about what I was planning for my contest entry, not telling my parents that I was going to help Katherine find her birthmom.

I thought about all the things I'd done and what I was about to do on Monday. I'd collected a lot of secrets lately, but maybe I hadn't really told out-and-out lies:

1) Nana's camera-I didn't lie exactly. I just didn't tell my parents I was bringing it, so that's a big difference. Besides, I had to bring it to take special enough photos to win the contest.
2) Sneaking out of the hotel room when my parents are sleeping -They haven't found out about it, and finding adventure is one of my goals, so this one's okay, isn't?

I chewed on a strand of hair. This next one was really bothering me, but maybe if I wrote it down it wouldn't sound so awful.

3) Lying to Katherine-I told her Plan B instead of Plan A, so this is only half a lie, right? Also, after I take the pictures I wouldn't actually enter the contest without telling her first, so that makes it only a quarter of a lie or even less.

I put my pen down, reading over what I'd written. Here's the thing: when Katherine first asked me, maybe the first reason I said "I'm in!" was because I knew it could be a winning entry.

But it wasn't like that anymore.

Now I'd help her even if there wasn't a contest. Because helping Katherine find her birthmom was something that could change her life, and I wasn't about to let her down.

I picked up my pen and finished my diary entry.

As far as secrets go, it's the sneakiest thing I've ever done. I'll be going out into a foreign city, not just hanging around the hotel, and we're not telling my parents or Katherine's. So that makes it even worse.

But I know that helping Katherine is the right thing to do. Her parents don't want her to try to contact her birthmom even though she needs to. If I'd been adopted, no matter how much I loved my parents, I'd still want to know where I came from.

Okay, so I've spilled. The hardest part about secrets is keeping them to yourself. Plus, the sneaking around is making me feel funny inside.

All I can hope for is that it works out the way I want it to in the end. Then it will be worth it, even if I have to tell some lies along the way.

Love,
Emily
(who feels a little better now that she's written down all her secrets)

"I've decided we should take a cab," Katherine told me Sunday afternoon as we stood in the game room that over-looked the pool.

"After we get back from the Embassy tomorrow?"

Katherine nodded. "I'll tell my parents I'm going swim-ming with you, and you can tell your parents you'll be with me. We can go to the pool when we get back so bring your swim bag. That way, even if we get caught we can just say we wanted to go to the pool by ourselves. We wouldn't get in too much trouble for that."

"So, what happens if my parents call your parents to talk to me?"

"Can you borrow your mom's phone? Then they can call and talk to you directly instead of phoning my parents."

"I can try," I told her. "But they might call your parents anyway. You never know."

"Well," Katherine said, putting a Chinese coin in the pin-ball machine, "it's too bad you didn't bring your cell phone like I did."

"My parents said I can't have a phone until I'm thirteen," I said. "So, there's nothing I can do about that. But Katherine, even if we pull this taxi thing off, what if your birthmom con-tacts you? You'll have to tell your parents the truth then."

Katherine hit the flippers. I watched the ball shoot off in different directions, pinging this way and that. Finally, it slid out of range and she turned to me. "I won't have to tell my parents anything until *after* I meet my birthmom. Then they'll finally understand they should have listened to me. They'll feel bad that I had to figure things out on my own because they wouldn't help, so I don't think they'll get mad that I broke a few rules, do you?"

I shrugged. I wasn't feeling as confident as Katherine. As much as I wanted to use the photos for the contest, I knew things could go wrong in so many ways.

Katherine snapped her fingers. "I've got it! If my parents ask me how I got in touch with my birthmom, I'll say I paid someone to put the sign up in my finding spot. I can speak Mandarin, so it's something I could have done."

"Maybe you should," I said, looking down at my feet. "Pay someone to put the sign up, I mean."

"No way." Katherine grabbed my arm. "I can't take the chance. Emily, I only have a few days to make this work! I can't trust a complete stranger to post my letter for me. I have to do this myself."

"I know. It's just—I could get in a lot of trouble if my parents find out."

"They won't. I promise," Katherine said. "If your parents call mine and find out you're not where you said you'd be, they'll call me. And I'll just say there was something I wanted to buy at one of the shops and we wanted to go by ourselves.

Shamian Island's a pretty safe place. I mean, they might get angry about it, but we don't have to tell them we took a cab into the city. And when I find my birthmom, I won't mention that you helped me. It's our secret, okay?"

I nodded. "Okay."

"Oh, you are such a great friend," Katherine said, throwing her arms around me. "Everything's going to work out just fine. I'm sure of it."

CHAPTER EIGHTEEN

Guangzhou, China, Day 8, 4/10/14
Dear Diary,
This morning we are going to the American
consulate to finalize the adoption. And this
afternoon we are going on the grand adventure
of my life.
    My stomach is a pile of squirming eels.

                                         Love,
                                         Emily

The noisy room at the consulate was full of people and their adopted babies, and it was another morning full of waiting. All I could think about was what was going to happen that afternoon, which made the waiting even worse.

Finally, Katherine and I made our getaway to the bathroom, so we could talk. After we reviewed the plans for the umpteenth time, I washed my hands and glanced in the mirror. Mom had made me wear a skort and nice shirt for the occasion. "It's not every day your sister becomes a U.S. citizen," she'd said.

Even Dad was wearing khakis and a shirt with a collar instead of his usual shorts and T-shirt. The rest of the people in our travel group looked more dressed up, too, so I guess Mom knew what she was talking about.

"I'll fix your hair," Katherine offered as we headed back out. "It'll give us something to do while we wait."

"Can you fix it like yours?" I asked. Katherine had French braids on the sides, but the rest of her hair hung loose down her back.

"Sure," Katherine said with a smile, but when we got to the waiting room there weren't any empty seats. Mom was pushing Mei Lin around in the stroller, trying to keep her busy, and another group must have arrived because the place was overflowing.

"I better go," Katherine said when Mrs. Bresner called Katherine over to help with Madison, who was crying. She linked pinkies with mine before saying, "See you after lunch!"

I nodded, my stomach twisting as I realized that in just a few hours, Katherine and I would be out on our own in

China, and our parents would have no idea where we were. My mind reeled with all the scary things that could happen to us and all the ways the plan could fall to pieces.

Finally, our names were called with about fifty others and we moved to another room where everyone had to recite something and then sign some more papers. And then it was done.

Mei Lin was an official United States citizen.

We piled back in the van, heading to the hotel for lunch. There was no more time for private conversations, but Katherine and I managed a wave as we got off the van and headed to our rooms. I could barely swallow down my usual lunch of peanut butter crackers. While Mom and Dad chattered on about our morning, I checked to see if I had everything I needed in my backpack. Pens and paper. My journal. Nana's camera. Important phone numbers like the cab, bus station, and the police. Some extra Chinese money I'd slipped out of Dad's wallet when he wasn't looking.

You could never be too prepared.

Then I threw in my swimsuit and towel, zipped up my backpack, and waited until Mom got busy cleaning up Mei Lin. I tried to pick just the right time, when Mom was focused on getting Mei Lin ready for a nap, before I said, "I'm taking your cell phone, so you can call me if you need to, okay?"

"Okay." I watched Mom as she tried to change Mei Lin, who was wiggling all over the place.

"I'll be back in a little while," I said, picking up my backpack.

"Be back by three," Mom said without looking up. "There's all kinds of nice shops we can walk to around here after Mei Lin's nap. "

"Okay." I hesitated, my hand on the doorknob. I looked over at my mom, her reddish curls pulled back in a pony-tail like mine. I thought about how both of us loved to play Scrabble, our favorite dessert was a Chipwich—two big choc-olate chip cookies with little chocolate chips all around the ice cream filling—and neither of us liked scary movies or riding on big rollercoasters. I remembered the story she'd told me about being on bed rest when she was pregnant, the way both of my parents cried when I was born.

I felt bad about the lies and sneaking out, but as I watched my mom getting Mei Lin ready for a nap, I knew without a doubt that I was doing the right thing.

"Love you!" I called out, then pushed open the door and stepped out into the hallway, ready for the biggest adventure of my life.

***

"Oooh, I can't believe we are really doing this!" Katherine squealed with excitement as we walked out of the White Swan Hotel and down the sidewalk, which was filled with tourists and business people. Shamian Island was totally different from

Changsha, where no one spoke English and no one had hair like mine.

"Lots of people from all over the world stay on Shamian Island because of the US Embassy," Dad had explained when we first arrived. Last night we ate burgers and fries at a restaurant that had checked tablecloths and a jukebox that reminded me of a place at home called The Hop.

"Did you get your Mom's cell phone?" Katherine asked, and I held it up.

Katherine checked her back pocket for her pink phone, then said, "Okay, we're all set. I called a cab, and we're supposed to meet it in approximately ten minutes at Shamian 4th and North."

I nodded, not sure I could get any words out. I race-walked alongside Katherine, and sure enough, as we turned the corner I spotted the green cab waiting for us just as planned. "Let's go!" she said, grabbing my hand as we sped down the sidewalk.

"Guangzhou Park," Katherine stated clearly, giving the address as we settled into the backseat.

"What are you two girls doing, off on your own in big city like this?" A Chinese man looked back at us in the rearview mirror and grinned. I immediately felt better knowing he spoke English, but Katherine looked annoyed.

"Our parents trust us," she said sharply. "And we have cell phones and all the appropriate numbers , including the police."

The man laughed and Katherine rolled her eyes at me. "Where are you ladies from?" Taxi Man asked us.

"I'm from New Jersey and she's—"

"We're visiting relatives on the island," Katherine interrupted then looked at me and put her fingers to her lips. I wasn't sure why she was being so secretive. "So how much longer do you think it will take?"

"It's only a ten-minute ride once we get over the bridge."

Once we'd crossed the river, the scenery completely changed. We'd gone from a small tourist town with streets lined with shops and restaurants to a bustling city with highways that looped underneath themselves. "Wow," I exhaled.

"Guangzhou has population of eight and a half million," Taxi Man said.

"That's bigger than New York!" I said.

Katherine shot me a warning look, as if I'd just given away an important detail.

"You never answered. What are you girls doing in the big city?" Taxi Man asked for the second time.

"We want to visit the park," I answered, and when Katherine didn't stop me, I added, "We heard it was a nice one."

"You are right about that. And here we are!" We pulled up to the entrance and stopped. Taxi Man announced the fare and Katherine counted out the money.

"Can you come back in thirty minutes?" Katherine asked him.

"Normally, I say you call another cab. But for two nice girls like you, I will be back in thirty minutes, at the entrance."

"Thank you," we both said, scrambling out of the car. It was a park shaded with huge trees, the path lined with miniature twisted trees in pots and plenty of bronze statues. Crowds of people made their way on a path surrounding a large lake.

The cab made a U-turn and drove off, leaving us standing at the park entrance, alone in a city of 8.5 million. I took a deep breath, then reached for Mom's phone. It had been seventeen minutes since I'd walked out of our hotel room.

Before I could even reach for my camera, Katherine said, "We need to find the message board," and took off at high speed.

"Message board? Hey, wait up!" I ran to catch up with her. "How do you know there's a message board?"

"Most parks have them. Besides, that's where my finding spot is—by the first shelter, which should be somewhere close by."

"There's shelters up ahead," I said, pointing to some picnic areas off to the side of the path.

We stopped at the first one where a group of old men sat at tables playing a game with tiles, but we didn't see a message board or a sign saying the number of the shelter. "What are they doing?" I asked as I remembered I was supposed to be taking pictures.

"Mah-Jongg," Katherine said. She was so busy looking around she didn't notice when I turned the camera on her.

"We should put up your note here even if it doesn't say Shelter #1," I suggested. "You could tack it to the post."

Katherine paused, then shook her head. "No, it has to be the right place."

"Maybe there's more than one entrance," I said. "We might be on the wrong side of the park."

"Good point! Let's go ask someone," Katherine said. She plunged herself into the middle of the crowd and began stopping strangers to ask them about the shelter.

For the next few minutes, Katherine spoke in rapid Mandarin to everyone we passed while I took some great shots of crowds of people walking around the lake. I had to be on the lookout for unexpected beauty, because even though we'd started off on our adventure, there was no way of knowing how it was going to end up. Plan B could come in handy.

Finally, a woman pushing a baby in a stroller nodded and pointed off to the left. Katherine turned to me and yelled, "Come on, let's go!"

So, I followed her as she pushed her way past the groups of people gathered on the path around the lake. As we neared the edge of the park by a clump of trees, I saw a post with the number one on it. "This is it!" Katherine exclaimed as she bent down and pulled a flier and a plastic container full of thumbtacks out of her bag.

"Good thinking," I said as she tacked multiple fliers onto the posts of the shelter.

Katherine didn't respond. She stood up and looked around, then hiked the bag up on her shoulder and took off again. "Hold up!" I yelled. "Don't you think we should post a few more"—"

My voice trailed off as I noticed where she'd stopped. In front of a small building up ahead, maybe the park offices, stood a large message board. Katherine just stood there staring at it, without reaching for her fliers.

"You found it!" I said. "What are you waiting for? Let's cover the board with fliers!"

When Katherine didn't make a move, I took a better look at her. She wasn't looking at the message board. She was staring at the grass below it. "Katherine?"

She sunk to the ground, running her hand over the grass. "This is where she left me," she said quietly.

I just stood there, not knowing what to say. I reached for Nana's camera, but I froze as I looked at Katherine through the lens, the way she was staring down at the grass, a look in her eyes I'd never seen before. Despair. Overwhelming sadness. Loss. Her eyes were filled with a kind of pain I would never know, the kind that comes from realizing your mother—the person who was supposed to love you and keep you safe—had abandoned you in the exact spot where you were now standing.

I put my camera down. I knew that photographers had to be tough, that they had to take photos of things they didn't want to see. My grandmother had told me about the time she took pictures of animals who had been hunted in big game contests: lions, leopards, elephants, giraffes. How difficult it had been to stare into the eyes of a majestic animal whose life had been cut short by someone for sport.

"But a photographer's job is to show the truth," Nana had said. "Because people need to know about the bad . . . and the good in the world."

Watching my friend as she sat on the grass, I knew I was facing a truth I'd never known before our trip to China. But it was Katherine's truth and I knew in my heart that I didn't have the right to share it.

I'm not sure how long I waited in silence, but finally Katherine got to her feet.

That's when I reached for my phone to check the time. "The cab's going to be back in ten minutes," I told her. "We need to hurry."

Katherine nodded. For the first time since I'd met her, she seemed like she was in a daze. So, I reached for her bag and began tacking the fliers all over the message board.

"What does it say?" I asked her.

Katherine shrugged. "Nothing much. Just that I'm doing okay, and I want to meet her."

I looked at the photos. One of them was a picture of twelve-year-old Katherine and the other was a small black and white photo of a tiny baby. "Is that your finding ad?" I asked.

Katherine nodded. "That's how I looked the last time she saw me."

We stared at the fliers a little longer, then I touched her on the arm. "We really need to go, Katherine," I said.

"Okay," she said. We raced to other side of the park to find a green cab waiting for us.

"You want me to put up a few more fliers at this end of the park, just in case?" I asked as we neared the taxi.

Katherine shook her head. "It's in the right spot. She'll see it," she said. "I'm sure of it."

CHAPTER NINETEEN

Taxi Man dropped us back off at the same street on Shamian Island, as promised. I checked Mom's cell phone one last time to see if there were any missed calls then dropped it back in my bag.

"We did it!" I squealed before we raced down the sidewalk. "Can you believe we pulled it off?"

Katherine didn't say anything. While she was the one who usually took charge, it was up to me to take over and get the job done. "We need to get back to the hotel, change into our swimsuits, and jump in the water so it will look like we went swimming," I said. "Quickly. I told Mom I'd be back by three."

Katherine glanced at her phone. "We still have for-ty-five minutes," she said, but we didn't let up until we got to the front doors of the hotel. Then we slowed down, taking our time as we waited for the elevator to arrive to take us to the ground level, so we could make our way to the outdoor pool.

"We can get to the locker room from outside," I told her as the elevator doors opened.

"Emily!" "Katherine!"

Both sets of parents stood on the other side, and they didn't look happy.

Busted. We were totally busted.

"Emily Rose Saunders," my mother said, her arms crossed in front of her chest, "I am waiting for an explanation."

"The same goes for you," Mrs. Bresner said to Katherine.

Madison stomped a squeaky foot. Mei Lin squealed and reached her arms out from her seat in the stroller, like she was really happy to see me.

Katherine and I glanced at each other. I knew we'd talked about what to do if we got caught, but my mind had gone completely blank. I had no idea what to say to my parents.

"We, uh," Katherine looked at me, and when I didn't help her, she snapped back to her regular self, confident and in con-trol of the situation. "We went shopping."

"Shopping?" Dad repeated, as if she'd just said we'd hiked through a bamboo rainforest to take pictures of giant pandas in their natural habitat.

"Yeah," I said, my mind starting to work again. "We wanted to buy something special. And we couldn't tell you, because . . . because" . . ."

"Because it was a surprise!" Katherine said triumphantly.

"Yeah, a surprise," I said. "For you."

I watched my parents' faces carefully, and I could see the anger soften a little. Those curved-down eyebrows straightened a bit, and the frowns went back to lines. I knew a good thing when I fell into it, so I kept going. "I know we shouldn't have done it, but we just went to the hotel lobby, and we were really careful"—"

"I figured it was okay," Katherine said, "because you let me go to the shops in the lobby by myself before—"

"And I figured it was okay because I was with Katherine!"

We looked at each other and grinned. It probably wasn't the right thing to do since our parents were definitely not grinning, but wow! Mom and Dad might get mad that I'd been sneaky and that I'd explored the hotel without permission, but it was a surprise. For them! How angry could they get about that?

"So, exactly what is this surprise?" Dad asked. "And it better be good."

I felt my grin sliding away. "Um, well, we didn't buy it yet. But it was going to have your name on it—"

"And our names, too," Katherine added. "Something special for the whole family."

"Except we didn't have any Chinese money." Bingo!

"So yeah," Katherine said, "we kinda forgot about the money"—"

"After seven years at the Chinese Immersion School?" Mrs. Bresner actually sounded more disappointed that Katherine wasn't using her head than she was upset about us being sneaky. "Did you really forget you can't buy anything with American dollars in China?"

Katherine shrugged. "I wasn't thinking too clearly, I guess."

"We were so excited about the plan, that's all," I said.

"You should have told us where you were going, Katherine," Mr. Bresner said. "It was nice of you to think of us, but that doesn't excuse the fact that you lied."

Katherine looked down at her feet. "I'm sorry, Dad. I really am."

"Me too," I said. "We shouldn't have sneaked out without telling you."

There was silence for a minute. I had a feeling the Bresners had already forgiven Katherine for not telling the truth. I was in for some sort of punishment, for sure. But who cares? We'd posted Katherine's ad, we were back at the hotel safe and sound, and Mom and Dad would never find out what really happened.

"Emily," my mother said, her voice sharp as needles. "Is that *Nana's* camera around your neck?"

CHAPTER TWENTY

For a moment, time froze. I was positive the hands of the clock had totally stopped ticking. I stared down at the camera, which was clearly in view. How could I be so stupid?

I'd been so focused on our adventure that I'd forgotten a very important detail: *Put Nana's camera back inside my backpack, and zip it up tight.*

"Emily. We're waiting for an answer," my father said in a voice that told me he wasn't kidding around.

"Yes." I cleared my throat. "Yes, it's Nana's camera."

". . . And?" Dad said.

I avoided his eyes, looking out at the swimming pool. "And, I brought it with me to China. So, I could take pictures for the contest. Because, I really really want to win the contest, and a plain old digital camera isn't good enough—"

"Are you telling me," my mother interrupted with a voice that was slowly rising, "that you brought Nana's camera even though we told you not to?"

I nodded. "But I had to, Mom! Nana's camera is special—"

"That's right," Mom said. "It *is* special. It's irreplaceable. It could have been damaged, or lost during this trip, so we told you not to bring it, but you brought it anyway?"

"I couldn't help it! I needed Nana's good luck. I took good care of it. You know I wouldn't let anything happen to it."

This time Dad cleared his throat. Maybe I'd gone too far.

Mom turned to the Bresners. "I'm sorry about all this. Whatever's going on, it's clear that Emily dragged Katherine into it."

"She didn't drag me," Katherine said quietly.

I bit my tongue to keep from spitting out whose adventure it really was. Because the truth is, it was all Katherine's fault. If she hadn't asked me to help her, I wouldn't be standing in front of my parents right now with Nana's camera around my neck.

Right about that point, Mei Lin broke into a howl. And I mean a HOWL. It was the kind that could bust your eardrums. The whole time we'd been talking, Mei Lin had been playing quietly with toys in her stroller while Madison sat on the floor and played with her own toys. But Mei Lin had just dropped her pretend phone, and Madison had picked it up.

It was perfect timing. We were getting way too close to the truth. If Mom and Dad were furious that I'd disobeyed them by bringing the camera to China, I didn't know what they were going to do when they found out that: 1) I'd snuck out with Katherine and taken a cab to a park in Guangzhou; 2) I'd helped Katherine post a message to her birthmom even though her mother didn't want her to; and 3) I'd covered up the whole adventure by saying we'd gone shopping to buy a present to surprise my parents.

Oh, boy. Was I in a boatload of trouble.

Mrs. Bresner turned to Madison. "That's not yours," she said, picking up the pink sparkly phone and handing it to Mei Lin. She stopped howling. Madison picked up where Mei Lin left off. I didn't mind a bit. Busted eardrums were better than a discussion about how I'd lied.

"Looks like we need to go," Mrs. Bresner said, picking up Madison, who was turning red in the face from all her howling.

"We're not finished yet," Mr. Bresner said, shooting a warning look at Katherine.

"We're not finished either," Dad said to me as he pushed the stroller in the direction of the playroom. "We're far from it."

I nodded glumly. That's exactly what I was afraid of.

***

We didn't talk about it again until after a long visit to the playroom. I was on my very best behavior, following Mei Lin around and playing with her the whole time. We tried out every toy, from blocks to Dancing Elmo. I sang songs while she shook the musical instruments, followed her through tunnels on my belly, and even put her on my lap as we went down the slide.

I stopped to take a few pictures with Nana's camera. I still couldn't get Mei Lin to smile, but she looked beautiful peeking out from inside the red tunnel.

The bad thing about playing with Mei Lin is that it left Mom and Dad alone to talk. About me and my punishment, of course. Every time I glanced over at them, they were looking straight at me and they definitely weren't smiling. It gave me a weird feeling in the pit of my stomach. They'd caught me in a great big lie. What were they going to do to me? Make me stay close to them for the rest of the trip and no more hanging out with Katherine? Ground me for the rest of my life?

Just as I'd suspected, as soon as we made it back to the room and my parents put Mei Lin down for a nap, questions started flying again. I knew they were on to me when they said, "We want to know where you girls went sneaking off to this afternoon. And this time, we want the truth."

If I told the truth, I'd betray Katherine. There was too much at risk. If Katherine's parents found out, they might take her phone to keep her from answering any phone calls from her birth family. I just couldn't do it, not after we'd come this far.

"Katherine went with me to take photos for the contest. It was the only way to get pictures with Nana's camera, just like I told you."

"And you thought you could get winning photos by taking pictures in the hotel?" Dad asked. "You didn't go anywhere else?"

I hesitated. I knew the story still didn't sound believable, so I added, "We went to the park, the one right up the street."

"You're telling me that the two of you went to the park by yourselves, when you were specifically told not to go anywhere without us?" Dad asked.

"Shamian Island is a safe place," I said. "You said it yourself, that it's just tourists and business people who are staying here. You let me go to the park by myself at home—"

"Emily!" Dad said. "Don't you understand we're in a foreign country? If something had happened to you, it would be impossible to follow a trail, especially when you took off without telling us where you were going!"

Mom just kept shaking her head back and forth. Dad took off his glasses, rubbed his eyes, and put his glasses back on. And that's when it really hit me.

We had done something really dangerous. It had worked out fine, but the opposite could have happened. I could never tell my parents the truth or they would never trust me again.

I dropped my head and clasped my hands tightly in my lap, unable to look at either one of them.

"We are so disappointed in you, Emily," Dad said.

Silence. I let the words sink in until I felt them in every part of my body. If they were disappointed now, I couldn't imagine how they would feel if they really knew what had taken place that afternoon.

Mom didn't say a word.

"This isn't the first time you snuck out of the room without permission, is it?" Dad asked.

I shook my head slowly. Wow. How did he ever figure that out? Dad was like a regular Sherlock Holmes or something.

"Which means you've lied to us countless times on this trip," Dad continued.

"Only twice!" I said. Then I remembered the times I explored the hotel, by myself and with Katherine. I clasped my hands so tightly they turned white.

"We trusted you, Emily. We gave you the camera because we felt you were responsible, but now we've changed our minds."

I looked up. "Ch-changed your minds?"

My parents were both nodding. "That's right," Mom said. "We hate to do this, but you've left us no choice. We're taking back Nana's camera—"

My hands tightened around the camera, which still hung around my neck. "But you can't! It's mine! You gave it to me as a birthday present, remember?"

"Of course we remember," Mom said. She paused, as if choosing her next words carefully. "Honey," she said, her voice softer. "You did something extremely dangerous. Wandering off in a foreign city on the other side of the world . . ." she shook her head, "without telling us where you were. I can't even bring myself to think about all the things that could have happened to you. When we gave you Nana's camera, we were trusting you with a very special gift. Your dad and I have discussed this, and we feel the only way you'll understand the seriousness of your actions—"

I shook my head. "I'll do anything, anything! Ground me until I'm thirteen, make me give up computer privileges—whatever you say, but PLEASE don't take Nana's camera. I just have to win this contest—"

"Emily. The discussion is over." Dad held out his hand.

My eyes watered. *I will not cry*, I told myself as I lifted the camera strap from my neck and handed it to him.

"You're lucky we're still letting you enter this contest," Mom said. "Sometimes it seems you've forgotten the whole reason we're on this trip. We did not come to China just so you could participate in a photography contest."

"Forget?" Something exploded in me then, and the words rushed out of me like the fizz that pours out of a soda bottle when you shake it up. "How could I *forget* that we came to China to adopt a baby? We've spent every day in boring government buildings just so you could take a family picture without me! Getting Mei Lin has changed everything! You're so busy with the new baby that you never even noticed that I'd brought Nana's camera and was taking pictures the whole time. You never noticed that I snuck out because you were too busy napping when we could have been out exploring China—"

"Emily." Dad put his hand on my arm, trying to warn me that I was going too far but I couldn't stop.

I shrugged away his hand. "Or that I was busy making plans with Katherine. The only time you've noticed me at all was when some stupid lady wanted to take my picture. And you let her take it, when I didn't even want her to!"

"Honey," Mom said in a quiet voice. "I-I know this has been an adjustment for you, but it's no excuse for lying, or sneaking around and putting yourself in danger."

I crossed my arms in front of my chest, trying to keep the tears out of my voice. "You know what? Nana would want me to have her camera. It's not fair. It stinks! The whole thing stinks!" I yelled and then I stormed out of the room, into the bathroom, slamming the door behind me.

Mei Lin must not have liked all the yelling because as soon as I slammed the door, she started shrieking. I dropped down onto the hard toilet seat, covered my ears with my hands, and that's when the tears finally came.

***

After a while, Mei Lin calmed down and there was a knock on the bathroom door. "Emily?" Mom asked. "Are you okay?"

"Go away!" I shouted. It didn't matter what I did now. I was already in deep trouble, and I'd already been given the worst punishment ever.

I thought back to my twelfth birthday in February, when my parents saved the best gift for last. I'd pulled the purple tissue out of the bag to find Nana's camera sitting at the bottom, waiting for me. I remembered sucking in my breath, unable to believe that my parents would trust me with my grandmother's most prized possession.

"For me?" I said, my voice barely above a whisper as I pulled out the camera.

Mom's eyes were shining. "She'd want you to have it."

I ran my fingers over the black vinyl, feeling my grandmother's spirit reaching out from the camera, filling me up inside with her magic. With Nana's camera, anything was possible.

I could hear my parents talking to each other in hushed voices. "Well, we handled that really well," Mom said.

Dad sighed. "We're not perfect, Lynn. We tried to handle it the best we could."

"Maybe we're being too hard on her," Mom said. "It hasn't been easy for her, becoming a big sister after being an only child for twelve years."

I sniffled, loud as I could so they could hear me.

There was silence for a moment, then Dad said, "Maybe we should rethink this, give her a chance to earn the camera back. Her grandmother would want her to have it, you know."

I wiped my eyes and cracked the door then. I listened for a while, realizing there was this thing called Parent Guilt, and it was definitely getting to them. So, I took a deep breath and walked out of the bathroom.

"I'm really sorry," I said softly, sitting down next to Mom on the bed. "About the lying and sneaking around. We— Katherine and I—thought that Shamian Island was a safe place, and we didn't go far from the hotel. Also, I'm sorry about what I said about Mei Lin. I'm glad we came to China to adopt a baby."

Mom smiled. My words must have been exactly what she wanted to hear because next thing I knew, she had her arm around me. "We love you so much, Emily. Two young girls wandering off by yourselves in a foreign city . . . anything could have happened. You understand that now, don't you?"

"I won't do it again," I told her, and I meant it.

Mom looked over at Dad, who nodded. "If you promise not to sneak out again—not even to go somewhere in the hotel on your own—then we'll let you use Nana's camera for the rest of the time in China, with our supervision.

I threw my arms around her. "Oh Mom, thank you so much! Just wait and see what I'm going to do for the contest!"

"But we're still keeping the camera," Dad said, "At least for now. You can only use it when you ask permission, understood?"

I nodded and gave my dad a big hug. It was all working out! Even though I couldn't win the contest with "Adopted Girl Finds Birthmom in China," Nana's camera could still help me win with "China's Expected and Unexpected Beauty."

A joy filled me up inside as I thought about how I had the best, most understanding parents in the world.

And that's when Dad's cell phone rang.

CHAPTER TWENTY-ONE

O h hi, Shelly," Dad said when he picked up the phone.
Uh-oh. Shelly was Mrs. Bresner's first name. I searched
my brain frantically for friends and family members called
Shelly but came up with nothing. Zilch.

"They did *WHAT?*" Dad glanced over at me, then at Mom.

Mom started asking questions, but Dad shook his head,
holding out his hand to tell her to wait. Oh, the agony, pure
agony, of being stuck on the bed listening to my parents' reac-
tions. I tried to slink away, but there was nowhere to go except
for the bathroom, and Mom caught me by the wrist when I
attempted to get up.

Dad listened for a few minutes, then said, "Yes, yes, of
course. Thank you so much for calling. See you tomorrow."

Dad clicked the End button on his phone and dropped it on the table. Then he turned to me. "That was Mrs. Bresner."

"I know."

"Looks like there's more to this story than you told us," Dad said, his voice amazingly calm. "Would you like to tell your mother what you were up to this afternoon or shall I?"

"Out with it already!" Mom said. "What's going on, Emily?"

I shrugged, looking down at my hands in my lap. "I can't believe Katherine told them."

"The girls took a cab to a park in Guangzhou today," Dad said.

Mom reacted the same way Dad had when he heard the news. Her eyes grew wide and all she could say was, *"WHAT?"*

"Katherine asked me to help her! I couldn't turn her down, I just couldn't!"

Mom took in a deep breath then exhaled. "What did you help her do?"

"She wanted to find her birthmom, but the Bresners wouldn't let her look. So, I helped her put up a letter at her finding spot so that one of her relatives will see it."

Silence. For a minute, maybe two, there was complete silence. What was Katherine thinking, tell her parents? She had begged me to keep her secret and the first time she was cornered, she spilled everything. Not only that, but she'd taken me down with her.

I sat there waiting for my parents to yell and hand out more punishments. But when Mom spoke, her voice was quiet. "What did she say in her letter?"

"That she wanted to meet them. I don't know what it said exactly because she wrote it in Mandarin."

"Oh, Emily." Mom shook her head. I had no idea what she was thinking but at least she didn't sound like she wanted to kill me. "That's a pretty serious thing, looking for your birthmom. And in China, it's nearly impossible to make contact. That's probably why the Bresners discouraged her from looking."

I looked up at my mom then, looked her straight in the eyes. "If Mei Lin wants to find her birth family when she's older, you should let her do it."

"Honey, that's a totally different issue—"

"No, it's not! Katherine's parents should have helped her. It used to be impossible, but not anymore. Katherine did a lot of research, and there've been stories of girls who've found moms, dads, grandparents, sisters and brothers! Mei Lin has another family out there, and someday she's going to find them. She'll have questions, too." I glanced over at Mei Lin sleeping away in her crib, and I lowered my voice. "You won't be able to tell her about when you were on bed rest. You won't be able to tell her what time she was born, or how much she weighed. You don't even know the *real day* she was born."

"You're right." Mom reached out and squeezed my hand, then released it. "Mei Lin will struggle with some of the same things Katherine is struggling with." Mom paused. "But Emily, we would be very upset if she goes out and starts searching for her birthmom without telling us, the way Katherine did. You should have come to us. You always have in the past."

"But I couldn't! I made a promise to Katherine. You would have told her parents, and she wouldn't have been allowed to go. I was the only person who could help her—she was counting on me!"

Mom pulled her lips together and didn't say anything.

"You know what I think?" Dad said. "I think we all need a break. We could talk about this until we're blue in the face." Dad turned to Mom. "We can discuss this later, when we have some time alone and can talk about this calmly."

Mom nodded.

"In the meantime," Dad said, "who wants to check out the Thai restaurant up the street? I don't know about the rest of you, but I'm starving!"

I shrugged. I hadn't eaten anything since my lunch of peanut butter crackers, which seemed like days ago, but I wasn't sure how I'd swallow down a dinner with my stomach in knots.

Mom forced a smile. "Sounds good," she said. "Let me change Mei Lin and then we'll be ready to go."

CHAPTER TWENTY-TWO

Guangzhou, China, Day 9, 4/11/14
Dear Diary,
Well, things have really fallen apart over here. I'll
start with the good news: 1) Katherine posted her
letter at her finding spot! Hopefully her birthmom
will see it and will call her while we are still in China.
    2) I decided not to tell Katherine's story for the
        contest. Maybe I've messed up my chances
        of winning, but at least I don't feel like my
        insides have been tied in a knot that tightened
        every time I thought about what I was doing.
        Katherine deserves a true friend helping her
        for the right reasons.

Okay, so that's it for the good news! Here's the bad:
    1) We got caught coming back and told some
       more lies to try to cover things up.

2) Katherine spilled last night, and I am in the biggest trouble of my life. I am still waiting to hear what my sentence is, but I can tell it's not going to be anything good.

After Mrs. Bresner called last night, my parents somehow got themselves together, acting like everything was normal while we ate at the Thai restaurant up the street. We didn't talk about what happened, instead focusing on Lisa Wu's plans for tomorrow. But I wasn't even listening. I was too worried about what was in store for me and I tossed and turned all night.

Mei Lin woke me up at 5:30 like usual. I could hear her squealing and moving around, and when I took the blankets off my head, she was standing at the edge of the crib, staring at me. Even though I was worried about what my parents had decided about my fate, I couldn't help smiling when I saw her.

Well we're off to the buffet for breakfast, where for the first time since we got here, I'll get a hefty dose of punishment along with my waffles.

Love,

Emily (a liar and a sneak but a good friend)

A little while later we were seated at a round table at the White Swan that overlooked the Pearl River. I could see people swimming off in the distance and a man on a barge floated right past the window like he did every morning when we were eating at the buffet. Dad had explained the man was cleaning the river, digging up seaweed and kelp and piling it on his wooden raft.

"So, we had a long talk last night after you went to sleep," Dad finally said. I don't know how they managed that since it seemed I was up half the night. "I know we waited a long time for Mei Lin, and we didn't want to keep talking about it because we just weren't sure what was going to happen. There have been so many changes in the system since we put our application in and we knew there was a chance that adoptions in China could shut down altogether. We thought about switching to the Waiting Child program—"

"Why didn't you?" I asked.

"We considered it," Mom said. "You saw me looking at photos on the computer, remember? I explained about the Waiting Children, and how we could travel to China much sooner if we wanted to."

"Those babies deserve a chance too," I said, and as I said the words I realized how close Mei Lin was to a Waiting Child herself. If we hadn't adopted her, she might have been moved to the other program if she didn't gain enough weight, if she was a little behind with learning to walk and talk. "Some of them are going to grow up in an orphanage and never get a family of their own."

Mom's eyes filled and she put her hand over mine. "Your dad and I had a lot of long conversations. But in the end, we had to do what we felt was best for our family. And when the referral came, we were so thrilled it was finally happening that we didn't take the time to see how you were feeling about all of it. That was wrong of us."

I nodded and looked down at my waffles.

"Becoming a big sister has been a big change for you," Dad continued. "You've always been a go-with-the-flow kind of child,' and you seemed excited about the China trip. But, we got a little caught up in the whirlwind and somehow we missed the signs that you needed to process what was happening. And not just the fact that we'd be on a plane for twenty-one hours and would travel to a foreign country."

I didn't say anything, just spread the syrup around on my waffle.

"Your dad and I have wanted another child for a long time. You probably don't remember this, but we tried to have another baby when you were younger. I had two miscarriages, and after that, we decided 'to look into international adoption."

I bit my lip. A hazy memory floated into my head. When I was around four, Mom brought the crib back into my room, telling me I was going to be a big sister. There was a trip to the hospital, Mom sick in bed afterward . . . and after a while, the crib was taken apart and moved back to the attic.

"We've always dreamed of having two daughters," Dad said. "And now we do."

I glanced up at Mei Lin, who squealed and dropped her spoon into the bowl of steamed egg so that it splattered up into the air.

"We thought the trip to China would be a great experience for you," Dad said. "I know we promised to do a lot of fun things on the trip, but we forgot how much time would be spent doing paperwork in government offices. We also forgot how exhausting it can be taking care of a new baby. Your mom and I aren't exactly spring chickens, you know!"

"Speak for yourself," Mom said, shooting Dad a look.

I squirmed in my seat. Everything was getting all twisted up and I didn't know what to say. "The trip to China has been great," I said. "It's been different than I expected, that's all."

"We know your heart was in the right place when you decided to help Katherine," Mom said. "You've learned much more than we could teach you about what it means to adopt a baby from China. You've been thinking of things beyond the surface, the way we always hoped you would, and we're proud of you for that."

I looked at Mom, then Dad, who was nodding in agreement. Did that mean they'd changed their mind about additional consequences? Were they going to let the whole thing go because of complicated circumstances? Just when I got my hopes up, Mom continued.

"But even though you were trying to do the right thing, we still have to consider your behavior. You put yourself and your friend in danger, and you didn't tell us the truth about a number of things."

"So, we've made a decision." Dad cleared his throat. "Your mother and I have decided not to let you enter the photojournalist contest this year."

My heart dropped to my knees. "But—but—why not?" I managed to spit out. I'd been thinking about all the photos I could take during the rest of our time in China, and I knew I could win the contest with Plan B. All my dreams about getting the scholarship and proving to my parents that I was a serious photojournalist were disappearing into thin air. Poof! "You already took Nana's camera. You can ground me all summer, but please please let me enter the contest!"

Dad shook his head. "I'm sorry, Emily. We hate to do it, but we feel it's the only way you'll understand that you didn't just bend the rules a little. In this case, you seriously broke them."

I threw my napkin down on my plate and flopped back in my seat.

"We have five days left in China," Mom said. "Let's try to make the most of it, okay?"

I blew air out of my mouth, trying to keep my angry words inside.

"You owe it to your sister," Dad said.

My eyes teared up. Without looking up at them, I nodded.

"Good," Mom said then her voice brightened. "Today's a new day. I think you're going to love the folk-art museum."

I held onto my silence in protest, not even looking at Mei Lin when she made funny *Brrrr*-ing noises right next to me. I finished my waffles, though today they didn't taste sweet at all.

***

Katherine got on the van after I did that morning. She walked down the aisle, her hair hanging straight down her back without any braids or coils and she was wearing a pair of shorts instead of a dress or skirt. She glanced up at me and waved but didn't smile. Her eyes were rimmed with dark circles and looked puffy, as though she'd been crying all night.

I waved back but didn't smile either. Neither one of us made a move away from our parents as the van chugged down the road.

When we pulled up in front of the folk-art museum, I looked out at the black buildings carved with Chinese writing and artwork. Big oaks shaded wide grassy areas, and a path cut through with curving sidewalks. Children from the art school sat on the grass sketching with thick black pens.

Lisa Wu had finally picked a good field trip, a perfect place for pictures about expected and unexpected beauty. Not that any of that mattered now. We walked inside one building after another full of ancient art, pottery, weavings, and furniture. It was a pretty cool place, but it wasn't much fun without a friend to share it with.

Katherine kept running ahead but I was stuck behind with my parents. Dad wanted to read every boring plaque about the history.

We were standing in front of an old-fashioned weaving machine when Mom came up behind me. "Will you take some pictures?" she asked, handing me her camera. "Dad's too busy reading plaques and I still don't know how to work this thing."

I almost reached for the camera, then stuck my hand in my pocket. "That's okay," I told her. "I don't really feel like it."

"Oh, come on, Emily," Mom said. "I'd hate to miss out on photos of this place. Even if you're not going to enter the contest, you're going to regret it if you don't take pictures of the rest of the trip."

I just shook my head and stepped away from her, even though it left a burning feeling inside of me. Being grouchy was no fun. Arguing with my parents made me feel awful, but I didn't know what to do to make things right between us again.

And I was dying to talk to Katherine about what happened. I was sure she'd been told she had to stick to her parents for the rest of the trip, but it also seemed like she was avoiding me. Every time I caught her eye she'd look away quickly, like she felt guilty about getting me in trouble.

After Mei Lin's nap that afternoon, we walked in and out of shops in town. Everywhere I looked there were non-Asian people pushing Chinese babies in strollers. Which made sense, seeing how full the room was at the Embassy yesterday morning.

It had only been yesterday morning when Mei Lin became an official U.S. citizen. A lot could happen in one day.

I was thinking about Katherine, wondering if she'd heard from anyone in her birth family or if her parents had taken away her phone, when we walked into a shop to pick out a qipao for Mei Lin.

"Oh, I love this traditional outfit for Mei Lin," Mom said, holding up a red one next to Mei Lin. "It will look darling on her!"

"It's called a qipao," I said, breaking my vow of silence-unless-asked-a-specific-question.

Mom looked up at me. "Now how would you happen to know that?"

I shrugged, looking away from her. What did I have to lose? "Katherine told me," I said. "We looked at qipaos together."

"Uh-huh," Mom said but she didn't ask any more about it. "Would you like to pick something out, too, Emily? You probably already know this, but babies and their siblings are supposed to dress up and have their pictures taken on the red sofa in the hotel later this week. It's tradition."

"I don't want a qipao," I said.

"A dress then? This store has beautiful clothes at very inexpensive prices. Come on," she said, pulling me toward a clothing wrack. And that's how I ended up walking out of the store a few minutes later with not just one dress, but three pretty dresses in green, yellow, and turquoise.

After we shopped for a while, we stopped at a deli for ice cream. They had the same flavors as they did at home, except for a few interesting ones like green tea, ginger, and black sesame. Mom and I went for our favorite flavor, mint chocolate chip, but Dad decided to be more adventurous and chose the green tea. Mei Lin had vanilla, and she gobbled it right up.

We ate our ice cream on a bench in the park. It was in the big square in the middle, with sidewalks and shops on both sides. All around the square stood those twisted trees in pots, just like the ones I saw at Katherine's park in Guangzhou.

"Those are bonsai trees," Dad pointed out. "It's considered an art to trim the trees so they look like that. Actually, I read in a book that these trees originated in China, where they're called penjing."

Dad continued to ramble on about the trees, but my thoughts were a few miles away, at the park where we'd posted the message. 'An image of Katherine staring at the letter she'd posted on the message board flashed through my head. So did an image of the way she'd looked that morning, shoulders slumped, flat eyes without her usual sparkle.

I needed to talk to Katherine.

CHAPTER TWENTY-THREE

Guangzhou, China, Day 10, 4/12/14
Dear Diary,
Mom and Dad have crushed my dreams. I thought they were the most understanding parents but now it turns out they are the opposite.

Yesterday we went to a museum, and today's trip is even better-we're going to the Guangzhou Zoo! But it's hard to have fun when you can't take pictures, you're mad at your parents, and you don't have a friend to share the day with.

I need to talk to Katherine.

Love,
Emily (who is no longer a photojournalist)

The morning was spent exploring the carnivores, primates, and reptiles section. Katherine must have been under strict orders to stick with her family and they walked at a brisk pace ahead of us. By lunchtime, I was beginning to lose hope. The only time Katherine even glanced at me was when I called her name to say hello. She looked better than she had the day before, her hair in one thick French braid that hung down her back, and she was back to wearing a sundress and sandals, so that was a good sign.

If I'd gotten into trouble with my parents, I could only imagine what her consequences were. But I still didn't understand why she wouldn't even look at me or ask me to walk with them. It made it seem like she was actually angry at me, when it should have been the other way around. The only way she could have been angry with me was if she knew what I originally planned for the contest, but since I'd changed my mind and hadn't told anyone except my journal, I knew she couldn't possibly know.

So, I made a decision not to waste another minute wondering. "Can I sit here?" I asked when I spotted an empty seat on the bench next to her at lunchtime.

"Sure," Katherine said so I put my tray down and squeezed in next to her.

AWKWARD. That was the only way to describe it. I couldn't very well ask Katherine why she had broken her promise right in front of her parents, and I couldn't ask her anything else about it either. For the first few minutes, we sat munching away on our burgers in silence.

"So, Emily, what do you think about the Guangzhou Zoo?" Mrs. Bresner finally asked.

"It's wonderful!" I gushed. "They have so many different animals here. Like the white tiger! I've never seen one of those before."

"I can't wait to see the giant panda," Katherine said.

"Me too!" I said. And just like that, the awkwardness between us melted away as we chatted about the zoo, talked about the museum from the day before, and I even told her about the qipao and the three dresses we'd bought yesterday.

After we finished lunch, we walked side by side to the next exhibit. When the Bresners didn't stop us, we walked on ahead, far enough away that we could finally talk. That's when I asked the question that was at the top of my mind.

"So, I've been dying to know, have you heard from anyone?"

Katherine shook her head and looked down at the ground.

"It's only been two days. There's still plenty of time," I said quickly. "I mean, your parents didn't take your cell phone, did they?"

"No, nothing like that."

"I was so worried, Katherine. I thought—I mean, I knew your parents didn't want you to get in touch with your birth-mom. So, I didn't know what they'd do."

"They just said not to expect miracles," Katherine said. "And, I'm grounded when we get home for two weeks except for gymnastics and violin lessons."

"Why'd you tell?" I asked her. "You made me promise not to tell, and I kept my word. Then we get the phone call from your parents—"

Katherine put her finger to her lips then, as the rest of the group was catching up. We watched the brown bear cubs frolic in the sun for a while then raced on to the next enclosure, so we could finish the conversation.

"Well, I sure got in a bunch of trouble," I told her. "A lot worse than grounding. My parents took Nana's camera and they're not letting me enter the photojournalist contest, can you believe that?"

"Oh no! Emily, I'm so sorry! I didn't mean for anything to happen—"

"Well it did. So, why'd you do it? I told my parents we went down to the park to take photos and they believed me *until* your parents phoned and said where we really were."

"They just kept shooting questions at me. You don't know my parents. They knew I was hiding something and they didn't believe the shopping story and finally, oh I don't know, I got so mad at them for not helping me that it just came out. You have to believe me, Emily, I wasn't trying to get you in trouble!"

I didn't say anything.

"I wasn't thinking straight," Katherine continued. "It's like those people who get brought in and questioned by the police all night. Eventually they crack. And that's what happened to me."

I still didn't say a word even though I probably would have done the same thing if I had parents like the Bresners. They weren't the type to back down. But still, it didn't make me feel any better about missing out on the contest.

The group caught up with us again and we stopped to look at the elephants. After that, Katherine hung back and walked with her parents. As I glanced over at her, I noticed the blank expression on her face again, the mask I'd seen the night after the truth came out.

I'd missed the chance to make things better between us. I wasn't a true friend after all.

Instead of thinking about Katherine and how her life must have been turned topsy-turvy, I'd only been thinking of myself.

***

"Who's up for a swim before dinner?" Dad asked when we got back to the hotel. Mei Lin had slept in the stroller for the last hour at the zoo and all the way back in the van. Now she was wide awake, making all kinds of nonsense sounds as she pulled things out of the diaper bag.

I snapped the computer closed and ran to get in my swimsuit. Usually I was the one begging for a trip to the pool. When I came out of the bathroom, Mom had already changed Mei Lin into a pink bathing suit. A few minutes later, we headed outside.

"Look!" Mom said as she dropped her bag by the pool chairs. "I can't believe it! Is that actually the sun peeking out from the clouds?"

I looked up in the sky. Sure enough, the white clouds that had hung over us ever since we arrived in Guangzhou were drifting apart, and a ray of sunshine poured through.

"I may have to use my sunglasses for the first time since we arrived," Mom said as she dug in her bag. "And maybe even some sunscreen!"

"I think you're being overly optimistic," Dad said as he spread the towels out on the chairs. "Those clouds are moving pretty quickly."

I was staring up at the sky, wondering if the ray of sunshine was a sign of good luck, when it happened. A splash. And then Mom's panicked voice. "Mei Lin!"

I spun around and saw the blur of pink at the bottom of the pool. But instead of running over to help, I froze.

While Mom and Dad ran and jumped in the pool, I just stood there watching, as the scene unfolded in front of me. My legs had turned to cement, and I was unable to move.

Like it was some other family I was watching, instead of my own.

In a flash, Dad dove under the water and pulled Mei Lin out. She coughed and sputtered and began to wail away. Mom and Dad huddled around her, taking turns holding her, trying to get her to calm down.

Another family rushed over, the mom holding her new Chinese baby. The dad put a hand on Mom's shoulder, checking to see if everything was all right.

My breath came out in a whoosh. All of a sudden, the feeling returned to my legs and I started to move. Fast, racing toward Mei Lin. "What happened? Is she okay? Is Mei Lin going to be okay? Is she all right?"

"She's fine," Dad said softly, his face pale like the cloudy sky. "She's going to be just fine."

I looked down at the baby in my mom's arms, her cheeks red from crying, her dark hair dripping wet. "Are you sure? Does she need to go to the doctor?"

"I'm sure," Dad said. "We looked away for a second and look what happened! We've been worried about her motor skills, but your sister certainly took off quickly."

My sister. I stared at Mei Lin, the words echoing in my heart. Whether Mei Lin came from China or from my parents, even if she had a birth family waiting to meet her one day, she was still my sister. Forever.

Tears slipped out of my eyes and rolled down my cheeks. "I'm sorry," I said. "I'm so sorry! I should have been watching her, but I was looking up at the sky and—and—" I sniffed, trying to catch my breath. "And then when she fell in I just stood there. I didn't come to help at all!"

"Oh honey," Mom said. "We're the ones who were supposed to be watching her—"

"But I didn't help!" I sobbed. "I'm the worst big sister in the world!"

"Oh, Emily," Dad said, putting his arm around me. I turned and buried my head in his chest. "You're a wonderful big sister. This was not your fault."

I sniffled into Dad's T-shirt, trying to catch my breath. Finally, I pulled away and wiped my eyes. "I'm sorry," I said again, and this time I wasn't just talking about what had happened at the pool. I was sorry for everything: not paying enough attention to Mei Lin, lying to my parents, sneaking out in a big city, being a horrible grouch for the last couple of days.

"I know," Dad said. Mom handed Mei Lin over to Dad and gave me a big hug. I closed my eyes and leaned against her. Then I put my arms around Dad.

"Family hug!" Dad said with a grin. Mom wiped her eyes and we circled our arms around each other. Mei Lin had stopped crying by then. She looked up at me, glanced over at

Dad, then Mom, like she was finally putting it all together. Then she looked back at me and smiled—a real smile, the very first one I'd seen from her.

CHAPTER TWENTY-FOUR

Guangzhou, China, Day 11, 4/13/14
Dear Diary,
Something really scary happened yesterday.
Mei Lin fell into the swimming pool and almost
drowned. My parents got to her quickly and she's
perfectly fine now, but I just stood there watching
and didn't do a thing to help. It was like everything
was happening in slow motion and fast motion all at
the same time, and even though I heard the splash
and saw her at the bottom of the pool, I couldn't
get my legs to move at all. I guess I was in shock
and by the time I realized my sister could have
drowned, Mom and Dad were already holding her
and there were a bunch of other people around
checking to see if she was okay.
    The whole thing really shook me up and something
sort of snapped inside of me when I saw my

parents hovering around Mei Lin, who was coughing
and crying. I saw the worry in their eyes for
the first time, that parent worry that I thought
about when Mei Lin had the fever, but my parents
seemed calm and collected, but this time the worry
was in the tears in my mom's eyes, and in my dad's
wrinkled forehead and curved-down eyebrows.

Most of all, I saw something else. Something
that's been there ever since the first day we met
Mei Lin, but I didn't notice it until that moment.
Love. I know it sounds funny because how can
you see love? Well I could see it on my parents'
faces and in the way they were holding onto her
tight like she was their baby and they would do
everything in their power to keep her safe, and I
could feel it in my own heart when I finally made
my legs move and joined my family in a group hug.

It's one of those things that's hard to explain.
Like I said, something snapped inside of me after
Mei Lin fell in the pool. And up until yesterday
it still felt like it was my parents + me + a new
baby. A family of 3 + 1, but somehow... now we've
become a family of 4.

Love,
Emily (Mei Lin's big sister)

That morning we headed out to a pagoda for a special
baby blessing. Katherine and I were back to "wave but don't
smile at each other" terms, but I knew it would all change
as soon as I got the chance. We only had a few days left in
China. Enough days for a miracle. If there was one, I wanted

to celebrate with Katherine. And if it didn't happen, it was time for me to be a true friend.

While we stood staring up at the two-thousand-year-old nine-story pagoda with red doors and red flags all around it, all I could think about was what I needed to say to make things right between us again.

We had to take off our shoes when we stepped inside the building. Colorful flowers stood in pots all around us on the floor among the golden statues of a man with a huge belly; Dad whispered to me that they were called Buddhas. A black cauldron burned incense, filling the room with a strong, sweet smell and I sneezed. Then a priest came out wearing pajamas and asked the parents to hold their babies for the blessing.

The priest began chanting in a different language, maybe Mandarin, maybe something else. Soon all the babies were crying louder than the chanting and the ceremony was officially over.

Afterward we walked around the grounds of the pagoda, following a trail around a huge lake. Then we stopped at a large burning urn. We threw in yuan, which was supposed to bring good luck. I watched the smoke rise into the air, closed my eyes, and wished for a phone call from Katherine's birthmom.

Back at the hotel, I asked my parents if I could go talk to Katherine while Mei Lin was napping. "Since everything has happened, we haven't had a chance to talk," I told them. I wasn't sure if they'd let me go alone, but Mom didn't hesitate.

"We'll give them a call and tell them you're on your way," Mom said.

"Thanks," I said, heading out the door. I'd been thinking about what to say since the night before, but when she opened the door and stepped outside in the hall next to me, all the words disappeared.

I threw my arms around her. "I made a wish in the urn today," I told her. "I'm hoping for a miracle."

"I made a wish too," she said. "Actually more than one. It looks like one of them came true."

I gave her a puzzled look.

"I thought you were mad at me!" Katherine said as we walked off down the hall together, side by side. "I felt so bad about messing everything up—"

"It's okay," I said. "You couldn't help it."

"It's not okay," Katherine said. "You could have won that contest. I bet you're a really good photographer."

"About that contest . . ." I paused, as we neared the elevators, then began to loop around in the other direction. I hesitated, wondering if I should tell her the truth. I hadn't gone through with my original plan, so why did she need to know? But from the heaviness in my chest, I knew I needed to tell her.

True friends didn't keep secrets from each other. I took a deep breath. "I didn't just lie to my parents."

Katherine stopped and looked over at me. "What do you mean?"

I didn't know how to put a good spin on it, so I just came out and told her. "My entry was going to be about you. I even had a title, 'The Reunion in China: Adopted Chinese Girl Finds Her Birthmom.'"

Katherine clapped a hand to her mouth.

"I know. When we got to the park I changed my mind and I realized it was the wrong thing to do. So, I never took any pictures. But I've been feeling bad about it ever since I came up with the idea. I was going to ask you *after* I took the photos, but *before* I sent them in as an entry. But you have to believe me, I would have helped you anyway. I wasn't doing it so I could win the contest."

Katherine stood there in the middle of the hall, gazing out the hotel windows. I wondered if she was about to turn on her heel and disappear back into her room, never speaking to me again. In a way, I wouldn't blame her. Now that I'd said it out loud, even though I'd changed my mind at the last minute, it seemed like I'd been using her the whole time.

Slowly, she turned back around to face me. "And what were you going to do if my birthmom didn't contact me?"

"Plan B, like I told you," I said. "The Unexpected and Expected Beauty of China."

Katherine burst out laughing. I felt a giggle rise up inside of me too, and soon I was laughing along with her. When we finally stopped, I said, "You mean you're not mad at me?"

"How could I be mad at you? You knew you were taking a risk to help me and you did it anyway. You're a good friend, Emily."

And then we were hugging again and giggling as we made our way down the hallway.

CHAPTER TWENTY-FIVE

Guangzhou, China, Day 12, 4/14/14
Dear Diary,
Well I did it! I told Katherine the truth and we're
still friends. Really good friends. Something I
never expected when I first met her in the
airport.
   Lisa Wu says we can spend our last two
days any way we want to. I want to spend them
exploring Shamian Island with Katherine... and with
our families, of course!

Love,
Emily

After breakfast we gathered at the red velvet sofa on the
second floor of the hotel for the famous red sofa pictures.

Katherine and Madison wore matching qipaos. I'd picked out my turquoise dress and Mei Lin looked beautiful in her red quipao. As soon as we got everyone lined up on the couch, one of the babies started to cry, and by the time people started snapping photos, the whole group was crying. Mom tried to get a family photo of the four of us on the red sofa but by then Mei Lin had climbed off and was howling at the idea of being put back up there.

"It's okay," Katherine said with a giggle. "I think it's something about this sofa. I'm crying in the photo my parents took of me when I was a baby, too."

We spent the rest of the day visiting the shops on the island, buying more baby clothes and souvenirs. Dad bought a T-shirt that said Ba-ba in English with Chinese symbols beneath, which is the Chinese name for Da-da. We also bought nameplates for each of us, an artist carefully dipping his quill into the ink and writing the characters on the parchment. Then we went to explore the park in the center of the square.

This time Mom didn't have to ask me to take pictures like she had at the folk-art museum and the Guangzhou Zoo, where I'd refused because I was making a point. The point was supposed to be that I was mad at them for not letting me enter the contest, but all I did was make myself miserable and miss out on a bunch of good photos.

"Can I use Nana's camera?" I asked as soon as we got to the park with its canopy of trees and interesting statues.

Mom smiled and reached into her backpack. "I was hoping you were going to ask that."

I took control of Mei Lin's stroller, and Katherine and I walked ahead of our parents, Madison running on her short legs to keep up with us. An idea was forming in my head, a way to use all the photos I'd taken for the 'Expected and Unexpected Beauty of China' along with photos I was taking during our last days. I knew my parents had taken pictures during the trip too, and even though they wouldn't be good enough to win a contest, they were photos I'd use for my project. Because while I'd taken a lot of pictures of the interesting and unique sights, Mom and Dad had taken pictures of *us*. And while I might remember the silk museum or the bonsai trees at the park, the images would fade after a while and wouldn't matter so much.

The project I was working on was more important than a photo album of a trip to a foreign country, and it was going to be amazing.

Thinking about my project filled me up with happiness, but it was edged with a sadness, too. A sadness because besides my parents, the person I'd most want to share my project with wouldn't be waiting for us at the airport, making sure she was first in line to hold her new granddaughter.

***

Guangzhou, China, Day 13, 4/15/14
Dear Diary,
This is our last official day in China. I can't believe
it! So much has happened, and two weeks have
gone by so fast. Katherine and I are going to try
to make the day last as long as we can. Because
tomorrow we both get on different planes and
go back to our own lives, and who knows when
we will see each other again?

Love,
Emily (who really is a photojournalist!)

Our last day started the way the others in Guangzhou had, with a big breakfast at the White Swan buffet. But this one felt different because we knew it would be our last so I tried to eat extra slow so I could remember every bite. We went for a morning walk around the square at the park and visited one more store in the lobby. That afternoon, I headed downstairs to Katherine's while Mei Lin napped.

She stepped out in the hallway, closing the door behind her. "It's crazy in there," she said. "Dad has his checklist, and he's calling things out, and Mom can't find things, and Madison keeps crying because she wants to go to the playroom."

"I can't believe we're going home tomorrow'."

"Yeah." Katherine had a faraway look in her eyes, and she bit her lip. I knew she was thinking of her birthmom.

"She might still see your ad," I said. "She could call you after you get home."

"I know." She took a deep breath and tears filled her eyes. "Mom and Dad are going to help me. They said they'd sign up for the DNA registry, and there's an agency that can help."

"Really? That's great, Katherine!"

"Yeah. It's just . . . it's hard, you know? Sometimes I wonder, does my birthmom like to go shopping? Does she like fashion, and does she think it's fun to fix people's hair?" She laughed, but it wasn't a real one. "I mean, I love my mom and all, but she doesn't like any of those things. She shops by catalog, and she thinks fashion is a waste of time and money."

I nodded, not sure what to say to that. I wanted to tell her I was sure she'd find her birthmom, and that they would have a lot in common. But I didn't have any idea what would happen any more than she did.

Katherine was quiet for a minute, then reached into her bag. "Hey, I have something for you," she said, handing me a small box.

"You got me a present?" I opened the box and pulled out a bracelet made of red thread with red beads. "Wow. Thanks, Katherine."

"I made it myself. Do you know about the red thread?"

I shook my head.

"People say there's a red thread that ties the babies to their new families. Forever."

"It's nice," I said as I slipped the bracelet around my wrist.

"So the red thread means you've always been connected to Mei Lin, even though she was born in China."

I ran my finger across the bracelet. "Really?"

"Well, that's the saying anyway. I wasn't sure if you'd wear it, but I wanted to give something to you."

"I'll think of you whenever I wear it," I told her.

Katherine smiled. "So, I was thinking about that red thread. And I figured if it ties you to a baby you never met before last week but now she's your sister, then it probably ties us together, too. You know, since we both got our sisters from the same place."

"You're right," I said, looking up at her. It was weird how you could become good friends with someone you only knew for two weeks. And it was especially weird how you could meet someone who you think is so different from you, and it turns out you're a lot alike after all.

Katherine and I made our way to her room very slowly. "I've got an idea," Katherine said. "Let's ride the elevator to the swimming pool, one last time."

I raised an eyebrow at her.

"Come on," Katherine said with a laugh. "Where's your sense of adventure?"

"It kind of got left behind when I lost the camera AND the contest, remember?"

"Oh, come on," Katherine said again. "It'll only take a minute. They'll never find out."

"Yeah, yeah, I've heard that before," I said with a grin as we stepped on the elevator. We rode down to the swimming pool, but after a few minutes of watching swimmers in bathing caps taking lessons, we headed upstairs.

"You should come and visit me next summer," I said while we played Uno in the hall to get away from all the craziness. "New Jersey is a lot closer to Washington than China, and we're like an hour from New York City. We could go to the Empire State Building. Or the Statue of Liberty or the museum. They have lots of cool museums in New York."

"That would be so great," Katherine said. "And you could come to Seattle. We'll take you to the Space Needle and maybe we could go on a whale watching tour."

"Awesome!" I said, and we high-fived each other for the first time.

Our next game of Uno was interrupted when my parents came by with the stroller. "It's time for dinner," Mom said with a smile. "All the families are meeting at a hotel up the street."

"See you in a few minutes," Katherine said, waving to me before she disappeared into her room.

The hotel was only a few minutes away. Guangzhou must have been full of fancy hotels because this one was almost as nice as the

White Swan. Lisa Wu took us to a private room in the restaurant that had big round tables with spinning serving plates in the middle. All the families sat down at two big tables and then she ordered all kinds of dishes for us so we could try lots of different things.

The waiters set down appetizer plates of dumplings with ginger sauce, congee soup, steamed buns, cucumbers in a spicy sauce, and strips of fried snake.

"You should try the snake," Katherine said as filled up her plate.

"Mmm," Dad said after taking a bite. "Tastes like chicken."

I started to shake my head, but then I looked over at Mei Lin. She stood up on Mom's lap, shrieked, and grabbed a piece of snake off the plate. I wasn't about to be outdone by a one-year-old. So I put a piece on my plate, took one bite, and chased it down with the extra-sweet tea that was in front of me. "So . . . what do you think?" Katherine asked.

"Great," I said, pushing the snake to the side and covering it with a napkin.

A few minutes later, the waiters and waitresses cleared off the appetizers and marched out with one plate of food after another, which they set on the spinning wheel in the middle of the table. Rice, noodles, meat, seafood, tofu, vegetables, even fried pancakes with fillings inside . . . and all of it was good. Except for the duck, which I plainly was not about to touch.

By the time the waiters came back with big slabs of watermelon, I was stuffed. I was slurping my watermelon, something I'd miss as my nightly dessert, when Katherine's dad stood and tapped his spoon against his glass. He talked about how it was our last night together, and since we missed all of their previous birthdays, he wanted to celebrate with us now.

Katherine's mother walked in with a big birthday cake that said HAPPY BIRTHDAY YIYIANG BABIES, and everyone began to sing.

"Blow out the candles," I said to Mei Lin. She squealed and stuck her fingers in the cake.

"Do you think they celebrated in the orphanage?" I asked my parents. "Did they have a party for Mei Lin?"

"Well," Mom said, "There's a photo I saw that they told us was taken on Mei Lin's first birthday. But they didn't give her cake. They gave her a plate of rolls."

I looked over at Mei Lin. Her face was covered with vanilla frosting and she looked a lot happier than someone would look with a plate of old rolls. "From now on," I told her, "You'll have cake at every birthday, whatever kind you want."

Mei Lin let out a big squeal, like she knew exactly what I was saying.

After we'd finished eating, everyone got up to sit in sofas and chairs at the back of the room. The next surprise was that people started passing out gifts. Katherine and her parents were the first ones. But other families passed out special poems and cards to all the babies, too.

"Were we supposed to bring presents?" I asked my parents.

"We had enough trouble remembering to pack the diapers," Dad said.

Mom smiled. "Instead of presents, we can send photos when we get home. Between the three of us, I'm sure we've taken some good ones."

Katherine showed up with a present while I was thinking about my photos. "We ordered necklaces for all the babies," she said, handing a small bag to Mom.

Mom pulled out a golden heart necklace. She drew in her breath. "Oh, Katherine, it's beautiful."

"Turn it over," Katherine said. "We engraved the back."

I looked down at the words. *You're always in my heart. Love from your YiYiang sister, Madison AiWen Bresner.*

"Thank you. This is really special." Mom wiped her eyes and gave Katherine a hug.

I pulled out my digital camera and started snapping pictures. I took photos of all the families with their babies, of Mei Lin with the other babies, of the rest of the cake that sat on the table; you could still make out the words "Happy Birth" and "YiYiang."

Then I asked Mom to take a picture of Katherine and me. We stood with our arms around each other.

"Will you send photos?" Katherine asked when it was time to head back to the hotel for our last night in China.

"Sure," I told her. "I've taken about a million tonight, you know."

But Katherine shook her head. "No, I mean the ones you took earlier. For the contest."

"Okay," I said, eager to see the ones I'd taken of Katherine before we snuck out for our adventure, the ones I was thinking could have been used for "Unexpected Beauty." "I can send you some of those too."

"I'm really going to miss you," Katherine said as we hugged one last time.

"Me too," I said, looking down at my bracelet. Even though we lived on opposite sides of the country, I knew in my heart that the red thread would always connect us in a special way.

CHAPTER TWENTY-FIVE

Guangzhou, China, Day 14, 4/16/14
Dear Diary,
It's still dark outside, but I'm in the van, on the way
to the airport. That's because it's only 5:30 in the
morning! Even Mei Lin didn't like being woken up
so early and having to pile all our suitcases on a
luggage rack and leave the room we've been in
for the past week without even getting to stop
at the buffet for breakfast. She started crying
as soon as she woke up, and she's not in a very
good mood right now, that I can tell you.
   It feels weird to be on the highway, moving
further and further away from Shamian Island
with its little shops and tree-lined parks, away
from the big buildings that form Guangzhou's
skyline, moving closer and closer to the airport
that will take us away from Mei Lin's homeland

and bring us closer to her new home.

Maybe Mei Lin doesn't understand what's happening to her and she's just grouchy because we woke her up early and we're off her routine. But maybe she knows she's leaving China and that's why she's crying.

Love,
Emily
(who will get to sleep in her own bed after a 21-hour plane ride, and is feeling pretty happy about that)

"I hope she calms down once we get on the plane," Mom said, giving her a bottle. That kept her quiet for a little while, but when she was done, she threw the bottle down on the floor and started howling again.

"I bet she'll like flying on the plane," I said. "The movement will calm her down."

"Actually," Mom said, picking up Mei Lin and patting her back, "babies don't usually like planes. Their ears are sensitive, so be prepared for a long trip home."

"They don't call the trip home from China the Crying Baby Flight for nothing," Dad said.

I didn't like the sound of that. Luckily, Mei Lin stayed busy eating Cheerios as we rushed through the airport. It was just like when we first arrived in China—lots of stops to show passports and get our bags checked. Finally, we stepped onto the plane. We had four seats in the middle, instead of an aisle seat near the window. What a bummer.

"Sorry, Emily. I wanted all of us to sit together, and this was the only choice," Mom said when I grumbled about it. She settled down with Mei Lin on her lap. But Mei Lin stood up on Mom's legs, trying to look over the seat at the people behind us.

"Are they going to make you buckle her in once the plane starts?"

"We'll see," Mom said, and that's exactly what happened. Mei Lin wasn't having any of it. She squirmed and shrieked, and Mom had to force her to sit back so she could snap the seatbelt. The engines roared as we took off down the runway. Then the yowling really started.

I pulled out a musical kangaroo from the baby bag and wound it up. "Look, Mei Lin. It's Waltzing Matilda!"

Mei Lin shrieked and pushed Matilda away. The kangaroo fell to the floor. The airplane started to rise off the ground.

"Say good-bye to China," Mom said, turning to the window.

I looked out the window on the other side. I knew we would make the trip again, maybe to post a letter at Mei Lin's finding spot. China was part of Mei Lin's story and she would need a trip back just the way Katherine had.

"When are we going to visit again?" I asked my parents over Mei Lin's cries. "Since we never saw The Great Wall, or Orange Lake, or a bunch of other places. Hey, we could come back in the winter, when they have the ice sculptures. I read about it in my travel guide." I pulled the book out of my backpack, but my parents were too busy with Mei Lin to look.

"Let's worry about getting Mei Lin home first before we plan our trip back," Dad said, trying to give her a pacifier.

I studied my guide, reading about all the exciting places we didn't visit, but Mei Lin spit out the pacifier, and a few minutes later, she was crying harder than ever. A man across the aisle shot us a dirty look and pulled a pillow over his head.

"People sure are grouchy around here," I said. It wasn't Mei Lin's fault that her ears were hurting.

"Don't worry about it," Mom said, patting my arm.

I pulled out Polky the Elephant. "Polky wants to say hello!" I said, but Mei Lin pushed the elephant away just like she'd pushed Matilda.

The seatbelt sign finally went off, and Mom unbuckled Mei Lin and put her on her lap. That helped with the shrieking, but she was still making unhappy noises and didn't look anywhere near ready to fall asleep. I tried shaking her rattle toy. She grabbed it and threw it on the floor. I pulled out a cloth book. She chewed on it, which kept her quiet for a minute or two. Then she tossed it like the stuffed animals. A bottle worked for a little while, until she drained it and threw that down, too.

I picked everything up and put it in the bag. Twenty hours was going to feel endless unless I came up with a plan, and quick.

So, I reached into my backpack and pulled out my camera.

***

"Wow," Mom said a little while later, when Mei Lin had fallen asleep against me. "Just like magic. You really do have the big sister's touch."

"Oh, it was nothing," I said. "Mei Lin likes cameras, that's all."

"I think she likes her big sister," Mom said, squeezing my hand. "I don't know what we would have done without you."

I smiled and leaned back against the seat. It was really pretty simple. Mei Lin liked to look at the pictures, and she liked to watch videos. I thought about my grandmother, and how I wished she were here to meet her new granddaughter. I knew she would have been the first one to greet us as we got off the plane, and the first to hold Mei Lin.

"Mei Lin's going to be a photographer when she grows up, just like me . . . and Nana," I said.

Dad laughed. "You've got it all figured out, don't you?"

"Well it's true." I opened my eyes and looked over at him. "So, about that trip to China. When are we coming back?"

"When Mei Lin's old enough to take photos," Dad said with a grin.

"And when she's old enough to understand," Mom added.

I settled back in my seat, enjoying the moments of quiet. Pulling out my journal, I read through My Fears About the China Trip one last time. It was funny how much had changed in only two weeks. I'd already checked off:

Number 1: What if the plane crashes?
Number 2: What if authentic Chinese food
            means the food will be terribly awful
            and I starve the whole time?
And

Number 5: What if I don't like Katherine and I'm
            stuck hanging out with her for two
            weeks?

Luckily, none of those fears had come true. And as I looked at the rest of the list, I realized that even though I'd experienced some of my biggest worries, I'd survived all of it.

I flipped to the bottom of the list, to the fears I didn't admit to anyone except my journal.

7) What if my new sister doesn't like me...and I
   don't care for her much either?

I looked up from journal, glancing over at Mei Lin sleeping peacefully on the seat beside me. When I wrote down

Number 7, I'd forgotten something really important: family meant a connection that could never be broken. I'd never had a sister before, so I didn't know what it would be like—the way finding out about Mei Lin's past had put a dent in my heart, the way one of Mei Lin's smiles lit me up from the inside.

I was a big sister and I would be for the rest of my life. Our family was different now, but

sometimes you don't know what you've been missing until it actually happens to you.

I shut my journal, thinking about my photo project. I wouldn't have an entry in the photojournalist contest, and I wasn't going to win a scholarship to the photojournalist camp. It had nearly crushed me when Mom and Dad first took Nana's camera away. I had thought I needed a magical transfer of special skills from my grandmother, an award-winning, world-famous photographer who'd used that same camera to take pictures for *National Geographic*.

Nana had been trying to tell me all along, but maybe I hadn't been listening. I had to find the magic within myself. I could take good pictures, with or without 'her camera. And I could follow my dream to be a photojournalist someday even if I'd missed out on a very important contest.

I couldn't use my China pictures to win a scholarship, but I could use them for something better. Something my grandmother would have loved. I closed my eyes, thinking about the video I was going to put together when we got home. I could feel the excitement building inside of me as I imagined my gift for the whole family. It would use all the photos taken in China, strung together with exactly the right music. I already had the perfect name.

Finding Mei Lin.

AUTHOR'S NOTE

In 2006, we traveled to China to adopt our daughter. At the time, orphanages were full of baby girls waiting for homes because of strict laws to control the overpopulation in the country. In the last decade, however, there have been a lot of changes.

In 2016, the law was changed from a one-child policy to a two-child policy. China has also tried to balance its male-majority population, finding homes for baby girls within their own country. Chinese orphanages now have many boys as well as girls available for adoption, and most are older children and/or children with special needs who are hoping to find families and a home of their own.

Because of recent events, I decided to add the dates to the journal entries to more accurately reflect the changes in the adoption process. While some places mentioned in the book are directly related to our travel experience, the names of many places have been fictionalized.

During our amazing two-week journey to Changsha and Guangzhou, we experienced as much as we could of our daughter's culture. Our tour guide from the adoption agency planned interesting outings for us, many of which are described in this novel. We visited beautiful tree-lined parks full of old statues where people gathered in large groups to perform Tai Chi and ballroom dances. We saw the contrast in this country, from the workers at rice paddies that we passed over before touching down at the airport to cities larger than the ones we have in the United States. People were friendly even though most did not speak English, and yes, our shy blonde-haired biological daughter had many photo requests from strangers!

When we first adopted our daughter, the agency told us we would not receive any information about her birth family. It was against the law to put a child up for adoption, so moms had to leave their babies at places where they knew they would be picked up and taken to the orphanage.

In writing about Katherine's journey to find her birth family, I 'read some fascinating and heartwarming stories about reunions between adopted children and their biological families. One story that stuck out in my mind was about a girl who (with her family's help) posted a letter on a message board at her finding spot in a park, and within days she was reunited with her birth family. In this book, I fictionalized the name of the park where Katherine posted her letter, though the description of the park was based on many that we visited while we were in the country.

After adopting my daughter from China, I was inspired to write this book to show how families can be different, but regardless of how they are formed, we all have common bonds of love that connect us: adopted moms and dads with their children; adopted siblings with each other; and adopted children with their biological families . . . even if they've been unable to find each other.

ACKNOWLEDGMENTS

I'll start with a huge thank you to my fantastic agent, Brent Taylor, for sharing feedback and believing in Emily from the start!

To Alison Weiss, for falling in love with my story and sharing your enthusiasm and excitement about the project. Also a big thanks for finding the perfect title and illustrator. Sending hugs!

To Jennifer Bricking, for the beautiful cover!

To Nicole Frail, for taking on the project and sharing your editorial wisdom. *Emily Out of Focus* is a stronger book because of your feedback.

Thank you, thank you, thank you, to the many writers and SCBWI members who have read different versions of *Emily Out of Focus* over the years and encouraged me to stick with the story. To Stefanie Gorin for your insight and enthusiastic comments on my very first draft. To Yolanda Ridge, for not only being a great critique partner through multiple drafts, but for being a supportive friend! To my sensitivity readers, Henry Lien and Karen Bao. I greatly value your feedback.

To Kathy of Wasatch Adoption Agency, for making our journey possible and for sharing updated information about Chinese adoptions.

To Liz, for celebrating with me during the happy times and being there (just a text away!) during the struggles. You're the best friend anyone could have!

To Naomi, for reading and supporting my writing- this means the world to me.

To Scott, for being by my side on this journey that started in China. I love you!

To Eliana, for being the best big sister ever.

And especially to Carissa (Lyric), Emily and Mei Lin would not be here without you. A red thread has always connected us!